MW01125232

Promise Me:
A Novella

Rivers Edge - Book 3.5

By Lacey Black

Promise Me: A Novella

Index

Praise for Trust Me
Rivers Edge, book 1

"Lacey Black is amazing with her debut novel!!!"
-Amanda of Crazy Cajun Book Addicts Blog

"This book had my emotions all over the place, I loved it."
-Author Ella Emerson

"This is a debut novel by Lacey Black and it was f*cking amazing with a capital A!
One of the best debuts I have ever read and I can't wait for more. She has gained a huge fan!"
-Sandra of Two Book Pushers Blog

Praise for Fight Me
Rivers Edge, book 2

"This was a hot, fun and emotional read."
– Sandra of Two Book Pushers

"It's another beautiful love story with a good balance of drama and reality based situations as well as showcasing Lacey's sterling reputation as an Indie Author on the up-and-coming list of one's to watch out for."
– Nicole McCurdy of Nic's Novel Idea

Lacey Black

"Can Erin get past her insecurities with Jake and his past treatment of her and embrace the undeniable connection that they've had since they first met when they were kids?
I loved reading this story to find out!"
– Lisa McGuire

Praise for Expect Me
Rivers Edge, book 3

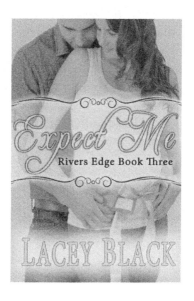

"I am a sucker for a romance with a surprise baby thrown into the mix. It always makes me smile. And the steam... oh yes, Travis will light up your kindle."
– Brianna @ Renee Entress's Blog

"I absolutely loved this book! I loved watching Joss and Travis grow together as well as individually throughout the book!! 5 Stars!"
– Kristin Marvin

"Lacey Black has struck steamy, small town romance gold with the third book in her exceptional Rivers Edge series. I am a huge fan of small town romances, and Expect Me is irresistible. Ms. Black has created a cast of characters that are all likable and relatable with plot lines that are realistic. She has mastered the art of drawing a reader into her story through her writing; it was impossible for me to not become invested in these characters and their stories."
– Danielle Palumbo

Dedication

To my editor and forever friend, Emily Getty.
This is way better than playing pretend school
while singing Bryan Adams.
"Everything I do, I do it for you…"

Lacey Black

Chapter One

Holly

"You are the luckiest beotch ever," I tell my best friend good-heartedly as she sits next to me in the limo while sipping a glass of champagne.

My best friend, Avery Jackson, is married to a hot, hunk of man candy. On top of his sheer hotness, he's a cop. Uniform. Badge. Hot.

"I am a lucky beotch, aren't I?" she states with a smirk from her seat next to me. A smirk and a far off look in her eyes tells me she's recalling a recent private moment shared with her man.

Tonight, we are celebrating Avery's twenty-fourth birthday. Maddox surprised her with tickets to see Bent, the hot rock band taking the country by storm, one concert at a time. Avery gave birth to my unofficial nephew last month, Ryder. He's perfect in every way possible. He has his daddy's dark hair and his mommy's crystal blue eyes. There's no doubt about it that he's going to be a heartbreaker when he's older.

"Not only did your hot-ass husband get

11

you tickets to Bent, but I want to know how he ended up with backstage passes, too?" I ask as I sip my glass of champagne, the bubbles tickling my throat as I relax in the comfort of dark, soft as butter leather seating in the spacious limousine.

"Jase's oldest brother, Coy, was stationed with Maddox and Jake on their tour overseas. They've kept in touch over the years, and Coy always said he could hook them up with tickets whenever they wanted. Maddox was only going to get the tickets, but Coy was able to secure the backstage passes and front row seats for him," Avery mentioned.

"Seriously. Lucky beotch," I say again and raise my champagne glass to solute the birthday girl.

"I'd like to propose a toast," Erin says from the seat in front of me. Erin is Jake's fiancée. Jake, Avery's oldest brother, and Erin are getting married this summer in the backyard of Avery's parents, Michael and Elizabeth. On the other side of Erin is Josselyn, Travis's wife. They were married this past Thanksgiving in their backyard mere weeks after giving birth to their son, Grant. I've grown accustomed to all of their deliriously happy smiles. I try to keep my jealousy in check since they've all overcome their own trials and tribulations to get to this place in their lives. Besides, Erin and Josselyn have become two of my dearest and closest friends.

"To our birthday girl, Avery. May you have another year of love, laughter, and hot sex. And when Jake and I finally start a family, I hope I have your body. You don't look like you just had a baby four weeks ago," Erin says as we all hold up our champagne flutes.

"Beotch," I mumble under my breath which causes the other three ladies in the limo to break out into another fit of laughter.

"To Avery," we all say in unison before taking a drink of the sweet, bubbly champagne.

"So, have you checked in with the guys, again, yet?" I ask Avery.

"Yeah, I sent Maddox a text a few minutes ago. He says Ryder is sleeping soundly and Brooklyn is playing dress up with Jake since Travis wouldn't let her dress up Grant," Avery says with a laugh.

It's hard to believe that Grant is almost six months old already. He is the spitting image of his dad with his blue eyes and sandy blond hair. Seriously, these Stevens' make the most beautiful babies.

Brooklyn would be my unofficial niece. Avery and I were nineteen when she was born. I managed to go to the local community college for nursing school, but Avery had to forgo college and get a job to support herself and a baby. Brooklyn's biological father is a Jerkface with a capital J. He had been cheating on Avery pretty much their entire relationship, and the moment she found out she was pregnant, he ditched her like yesterday's Chinese take-out. Drake Connor isn't worth the designer jeans and fancy loafers he wears.

Maddox stepped in and adopted Brooklyn within weeks of their wedding a year ago. In fact, little Ryder was born a year and two days after Avery and Maddox's nuptials. Avery finally has her happily ever after, and I couldn't be happier or more proud of the woman she has become.

"So, tell me about Doctor Paul," Avery says. All eyes filled with sparkly excitement turn towards me.

"He's a doctor?" Josselyn asks.

"No," I reply. "He's only a nurse."

"So, why do you call him Doctor Paul?" Erin asks, her beautifully manicured eyebrows raised in question.

"Because he struts around the hospital

acting like a doctor," Avery quips with a huge smile.

"He's nice," I defend.

"He's arrogant," Avery replies, and it's true. He is a cocky, arrogant guy. He flirts shamelessly with anyone with legs and boobs, and honestly believes he's God's gift to women. He's also the only guy to show me any attention lately.

I've dated on and off in the past couple of years, but have never found that person who challenges me. Who desires more than just a few romps in the hay - figuratively speaking. I'm not into sex in the barn. Hell, right now, I'd be happy with sex. Period.

Doctor Paul and I have been out on a couple dates in the past few weeks and have flirted brazenly in the hallways at the hospital, but I don't see it going any further than that. He's nice but definitely more into himself than he is into me. But it's not like any other young, single, good looking guys are lined up, anxiously waiting to take me on a date, so it'll do for now. It's better than sitting at home alone on Friday or Saturday nights.

I feel the limousine slowing before it pulls into the arena in St. Charles. I'm from Rivers Edge, Missouri which is a small town about thirty minutes away from St. Charles. Small towns breed gossips. If you want to know something about yourself, just ask around town. You'll find out plenty.

"Oh my gosh, we're here!" Avery exclaims, blue eyes lighting up like the Fourth of July. "I can't believe we're going to meet Jase Bentley," Erin exclaims just as excited.

I stare at the large arena where the Missouri Belters basketball team plays and feel the excitement and energy of the stadium zip through my body. People are everywhere. Girls wearing tight jeans and barely-there shirts. Guys wearing huge, cocky smiles as they check out all the bare skin floating around.

"Ready?" Avery asks me as the driver opens the door for us.

I step out into the cool April night and adjust my top. I chose a dark blue halter top that hugs my breasts just right. My brown, curly hair hits just below my shoulders and is usually pulled back in a ponytail or a clip for work, but tonight I decided to leave it down. There's just enough bounce in the big curls to give it a luscious, sexy appearance - at least that's what Avery told me when we got ready tonight. I stand along the limo in my wedge sandals which gives the appearance that I'm taller than my normal five foot four inch body.

"Ready," I tell Avery as we all link arms and head towards the front doors of the arena.

After showing our tickets to the girls holding the scanners at the front door, and having our purses checked by the big bouncer-like men, we head towards the stage where we're supposed to receive our backstage passes.

"I seriously can't believe we are about to meet Jase Bentley," Avery says excitedly.

"Me either! He's so friggin' hot," Erin adds.

"He's okay," I mumble. Three sets of eyes turn towards me. Eyes that are completely filled with shock and disbelief.

"He's okay?" Josselyn asks, eyes wide and mouth forming a perfect 'o'. She looks horrified, like she can't believe the two little words I just said.

"Well, he's kinda full of himself. I can't stand that. Yeah, he's good looking, but he knows it. He's cocky and arrogant and only dates supermodels and movie stars. I'd rather meet the drummer," I say with a shrug as we reach the front of the line to get our passes.

And part of that is true. Jase Bentley is all of the things I just said, but he also has green eyes the color of freshly cut grass and dark hair that's wild and slightly unkempt that gives him the appearance that he's just got out of bed. And his devilish smile will cause a nun's underwear to melt right off her body. According to all of the gossip magazines, he's twenty six years old and six foot tall with a lean, muscular body that he works daily to keep in his godly, chiseled shape. Both arms and most of his chest are covered in tattoos. He's the epitome of a tall, dark, sexy Rock God. Ladies swoon and the guys want to be him. Hell, I'm pretty sure half the fellas swoon, too. He's dangerous with a capital D, which is why I plan to avoid him like the plague when we get backstage. I don't need his kind.

Backstage passes secured around our necks, Avery, Erin, Josselyn and I step behind the heavily guarded curtain and in the bright lights of the backstage area. Girls are everywhere. I bet there are five girls for every guy back here. The line is long as we find our way to the end of it for the extensive wait. I don't see anyone out yet to greet the fans, only a very large, very muscular ex-lineman looking guy with his arms crossed over his chest and a scowl on his face inviting anyone to try to get past him. He's guarding the door like his life depends on it, and honestly, it probably does.

At seven o'clock on the dot, the door opens and members of the band Bent start to file out and stand in front of the signage promoting the band's latest tour and major sponsors. I hold my breath and wait for him to walk out. I told the girls that I wasn't excited to meet him and that I was only here to meet the drummer, but that was a boldfaced lie. My heart speeds up and my palms begin to sweat as I wait for him to walk out. And when he finally does, the noise of the room fades away. The dozens of screaming women evaporate around me. Jase Bentley walks out from the back room with his head down and a serious scowl on his face as if he's lost deep in his innermost thoughts. My eyes are fixed on his ripped up jeans that hang just right on his slender hips. His black t-shirt has the sleeves ripped off so that his tattoos are in full view. The shirt is tight enough to hug his muscular chest and show off the definition hidden underneath. He looks amazing. So much better in person than any of the photos in those magazines or his appearances on all the entertainment programs on television.

As if remembering where he's at, he gives his head a small, quick shake and lifts his eyes to scan the room. His green eyes are striking as they scan the crowded room filled to capacity with screaming, adoring fans. He plasters on his trademark bad boy smile which causes the screams in the room to reach eardrum shattering decibels. I watch as he struts up to the center of the room where the rest of his band waits for him. His eyes scan the crowd one more time and that's when the world stops spinning. Green eyes the color of dewed morning grass slam into me like a speeding Mack truck. The room starts to spin as he holds my gaze. The room, the people, the cameras all fade away until it's just me and those deep green eyes. I know in that moment that I'm in trouble.

Deep, deep trouble.

Chapter Two

Jase

Another city, another night of performing in front of thousands of screaming fans. It used to be my high, my drug. Now, it's just another night of fake smiles and forced appearances. When did this business become all about business and less about music? The music was supposed to *be* the business.

I stare at my reflection one last time in the bathroom mirror while the band's manager, Phillip Mitchell, continues to run his mouth just outside the door. I tuned him out about five minutes ago, but he apparently hasn't noticed yet that I'm not engaging in the conversation about tonight's tour stop. St. Charles, Missouri. Another city. Another stage. Another show.

Venues like this used to be my favorite stops on the tour. The smaller arena crowds gave a more intimate show. The fans were closer to the stage. But in the past three years, the venues got bigger and bigger. Bigger lights. Bigger displays. Fill the seats. Make the money. Money is great, but it's not the reason I do what I do.

"You about ready?" Phillip asks through the wooden door.

I give myself one last look-over and reach for the knob. "Yep," I reply as I step through the door.

"What's wrong with you lately? You've been distant and standoffish this entire leg of the tour," Phillip asks with the scowl I see firmly in place more often than not lately. I've known him for the six years that I've been signed under Cardello Records. Besides my bandmates, Phillip is the closest person I have to a friend anymore.

"Nothing," I mumble as I step out of the bathroom, closing the door securely behind me.

"Bullshit," he replies. "Something's up. Tell me."

I sigh a deep exhale. Maybe telling him I'm burnt out will help alleviate the pressure that's been constantly pushing against my chest for the past six months. "I'm just getting tired, Phil. I'm tired of cameras following me everywhere I go. I'm tired of the constant go-go-go."

"That's what you signed on for, Jase. That's part of it," Phillip counters.

"Yeah, but it didn't used to be like this. I used to love the fans and the crowds and the stage.

Now, it just suffocates me. Everyone wants more, more, more. One more piece. I need a break," I finally tell him, staring deeply into his dark grey eyes, hoping he can see the seriousness reflected in my own.

"You're living the dream, man. You have a smoking hot supermodel girlfriend. You have girls throwing themselves at you on and off the stage every night. Guys want to be you. You have more money than Donald Trump, and you're complaining?" Phillip says with a look of shock and horror all over his aging forty year old face.

"First off, I doubt I have more money than Donald Trump. And second, Camille and I broke up last week," I tell him.

"What?! How am I just now hearing about this?" he exclaims loud enough to draw attention from those standing around us.

"It was time. She wasn't into me for anything more than the fame I could contribute to her floundering career. She wanted arm candy and a name attached to hers for the press."

"So? She's fucking Camille Douglas. Freaking swimsuit supermodel. You don't break up with a fucking supermodel, Jase."

"Well, I did. I'm tired of the shallow and

the selfish."

"How is it that the press hasn't caught wind of this yet?" Phillip asks as he leans in and whispers so not to draw further attention to our conversation.

"She thinks I'll come crawling back to her any day now. She thinks I can't make it in this world without her. She's not going to the press because she thinks I'll be back. Well, she's wrong. I'm done with all that bullshit. I want normal. I want love."

"Love. What the hell do you know about love, Jase? This business doesn't have room for love. This business is filled with dicks that will better your career and tits that will help make it happen."

"Exactly. I'm tired, Phil. I'm not extending the tour again. I want some time off," I tell him as we make our way to the door. The door separates me from a room full of anxious, screaming fans. I used to love this part of the job. Meeting the fans and spending time with them, with those that bought my records and sing along with my songs. But lately, I'm just about as sick of them as I am the job. Everyone wants something from me. Including Phillip.

"You're just feeling down about losing

Camille. I'll grab a couple of girls from the show, and they'll help you get your mind back on track," Phillip offers with a big wolfish smile on his face.

In truth, I haven't been into groupies in the last couple of years. I haven't wanted temporary distractions or temporary relief from life in a while. I want more.

I watch as the band heads through the door to begin the Meet and Greet. I turn my attention towards Philip before I push through the door. "I don't need groupies, Phil. I'm perfectly capable of finding my own company for the evening if I so choose. And right now, I'm not interested."

"Suit yourself, man. Just let me know if you need a few girls to drop to their knees or spread their legs. Hell, they could do both – all together – if you want, Jase. Girls like that are a dime a dozen back here as you very well know," he says with a huge devilish smile on his charming face. Phillip has been known to take advantage of the never ending train of willing groupies backstage. It comes with the business. Just don't tell his wife.

I don't acknowledge his last comment, but instead push my way through the heavy door leading towards the Meet and Greet. I hear the screams and the hollers, but my eyes remain cast

Lacey Black

downward. I watch my worn black boots as I step into the room, through the crowd of people, and head towards the front of the room. *Snap out of it, man*. I give my head a quick little shake and look up at the crowd. Flashbulbs are popping like fireworks. I give the room my full-watt smile. It's a smile I've perfected in the past six years that brings the ladies to their knees. Sometimes literally. It's a smile that hides the pain that's within. I know that if I'm smiling, then no one knows the turmoil that's brewing and rolling like thunder from deep within my gut. No one knows just how lonely and miserable I really am.

I scan the crowd but don't register the faces. Blondes, brunettes, redheads. Girls, girls, girls, and more girls. All screaming, snapping pictures, and jumping up and down in their skimpy little outfits with their legs exposed and their tits hanging out. I head to the front and position myself in between my band mates underneath the big banner with our name on it, just like I do every night.

I skim the crowd one more time, but this time I actually take note of someone in the crowd. My eyes clash into a pair of stunning hazel eyes at the back of the room. My chest tightens and I struggle to gulp air in my lungs. Her eyes meet mine at the exact same time, and she's stunning. I

26

couldn't look away from her if I tried, and she seems to have the same reaction to me. She stares back, mouth slightly agape, and I feel the burn of her gaze from all the way up here. My body hums to life for the first time in months. Hell, years.

"Who's that?" Phillip asks as he approaches from behind and hands me a Sharpie, taking in the mystery woman in the back of the room that I can't seem to get my eyes off of.

"That's my future wife."

Chapter Three

Holly

"Oh my Gawd! Jase Bentley is staring at you," Avery says just over my left shoulder. I know Jase Bentley is staring at me because I'm staring at him. It's like I've been sucked into some alternative universe where only he and I exist. I feel so connected to him, all the way from the opposite side of the room. We continue to stare at each other until a slightly shorter man walks up behind him and starts talking. He stares for a few more moments before turning his attention to the man behind him, taking the offered marker from his hand.

With that, the line starts to slowly inch forward towards the five members of Bent. They are on the second leg of their coast to coast tour which includes stops at some of the biggest venues in the country. Bent stormed onto the music scene six years ago with their debut song "Fire", and they haven't looked back since. They toured with Katy Perry, Maroon 5, and Daughtry before claiming their own tour three years ago. Three albums and two Grammy's later, Bent is one of the biggest names in rock music to date. It doesn't hurt that the lead singer is drop dead gorgeous and has the voice of a God. Deep, throaty, and edgy. Sexy. A voice that makes panties burst into flames with the first word of any song.

Slowly over the next hour, we make our way towards the front of the line. The opening act, Hassle and Concur, is performing on stage, getting the crowd warmed up and ready for Bent. I'm completely fine with missing the opening act. Especially since I'm about to come face to face with one of the sexiest rockers in all of music.

I take note of the conversations around me. Avery, Erin, and Josselyn are all talking up a storm about babies, weddings, and the concert in general. I don't actively participate in their conversations, though. Instead, I people watch mostly, occasionally returning my eyes to the band at the front of the room. I watch as they sign shirts, CD's, posters, and even the occasional offered body part. Women throw their arms around their necks and grab at any part of their bodies that they can get their hands on. The band poses for countless pictures, their famous smiles never wavering from their faces.

It takes nearly an hour and ten minutes before we're finally standing at the front of the line. I didn't bring anything for them to sign, but I'm eager to get a photo with the band.

"I can't believe we're about to meet Bent," Josselyn exclaims as she bounces up and down on her sandal covered toes.

"I know! This is so freaking amazing," Erin adds.

Finally, it is our turn. One by one, the band members each turn their attention towards us. Each one has a Sharpie in their hands. Avery is at the front of the line and produces her backstage pass for each member to sign. I watch as she steps up to Jase and gives him a huge, fan-girl smile. He laughs at something she says before wrapping his arm securely over her shoulder. The rest of the band gathers around for a picture taken with her cell phone.

Erin and Josselyn each go next, securing autographs and photos with the band. I stand back and watch until, finally, it's my turn. I have no clue what each of the band members say because my eyes are focused on the lead singer. He's been staring back at me off and on during the entire Meet and Greet, but since I got up near the front of the line, his gaze has been constant.

I slowly walk towards him, willing my legs to keep me upright and not fail me now. Suddenly,

I'm questioning my choice in footwear. *Please for the love of all things holy, don't let me trip!*

"Hi," he finally says. Those deep timbers of his voice wash over me like a warm shower.

"Hi," I reply because, frankly, it's the only thing I can get out of my suddenly desert dry mouth, and even then it comes out like sandpaper. I'm like a freshman girl meeting the senior quarterback on the first day of high school. My knees are knocking so damn bad, I'm worried everyone around me will hear them. *Please, knees, don't fail me now.*

"Jase," he finally says as he extends his hand towards me. I take his large, warm hand within my own and feel the energy immediately. That warm contact is like a shot of tequila. I feel it burn my throat, warm my belly, and makes me tingle all the way down to my toes - including my dormant lady parts. They are definitely taking notice of the fine specimen of man candy standing in front of me holding my hand.

"Holly," I finally reply, my tongue darting out to wet my instantly dry lips.

"It's a pleasure to meet you, Holly," he says without letting go of my hand, his eyes diverted to my lips.

"Can I take a quick picture for you, honey?" the young man whose job it was to snap the dozens and dozens of fan photos asks as he reaches his hand forward for my cell phone.

"Sure," I reply, producing my phone from my back pocket.

I turn to face the guy and feel the strong arm of Jase Bentley reach around my shoulder, pulling me snuggly against his hard body. Cheese and rice, this man is firm in the best possible way and smells amazing. I have to restrain myself from leaning over just a little, inhaling his musky scent, and licking his neck. I uncontrollably shudder at the contact of his body firmly against mine - or from the images dancing through my warped, perverse mind. I wrap my arm securely around his waist and somehow manage to smile for the camera.

After the photo is taken, I feel his warm breath against the top of my head, warming my already flush face. Neither one of us have let go yet even though the photo was taken several seconds ago, so I slowly turn towards him, still securely in his deep embrace. He's staring down at me, mouth slightly open as if wanting to say something but not quite sure what to say. His eyes dance with question and maybe - what? Desire?

Well, that can't be it. Could it?

"Excuse me, but could we take a quick picture of all of us together with the band?" Avery asks the bored guy who was taking pictures.

"Sure thing, honey," he replies with an instant smile that borders on creepy.

Avery, Erin, and Josselyn all weave their way in between the band members. Jase never moves his arm from around my shoulder, nor do I move my arm from around his waist. It feels too good, too secure, too right. *Down girl!*

After the photo, the girls all engage in friendly conversation with the band since we were the last ones in line for the Meet and Greet. Jase turns his attention back to me. "So…" he starts.

"So…" I reply.

"What brings you here tonight?" he asks but then he seems to register the stupidity of his question. "Sorry. I guess that's an obvious answer, huh?" he says with a hearty laugh. A beautiful laugh. It seems so real and genuine and lights up his entire face.

I smile at his ability to poke fun at himself. "My friend, Avery, over there - the blond - it's her birthday tomorrow. Her husband got us tickets."

"Yeah? Nice husband," he responds with

33

another award-winning smile.

"Actually, I think he got the tickets from your brother."

Jase raises an eyebrow in question. "Which one?"

"Coy, maybe? He was in the same unit as Maddox and Jake, I guess, in the military," I reply.

"Oh yeah. Coy called me a couple of weeks ago for four tickets. Are you married to one of them?" he asks as green, hopeful eyes staring back at me while he awaits my answer.

"Oh, no. Avery is married to Maddox and Jake is her brother. Jake is engaged to Erin, the redhead over there," I say as I point to Erin. "And Josselyn is married to Avery's youngest brother, Travis."

"So, married, married, and engaged. What about you? Are you married or engaged?" Jase asks, trying his best to pull off casual, but it comes off slightly overzealous.

"No," I manage to respond only a fraction of a second before the man from earlier walks up and interrupts us.

"Jase, time to go on," he says with a slap on the back.

"Thanks, Phil," Jase responds and turns his attention back to me.

"Well, we better get out to our seats," I finally say as I stare back at green eyes.

"I -" he starts and then stops. "I was wondering if you would come backstage after the show and hang out for a bit," he finally says in one quick breath. I notice he's holding his breath as if nervously awaiting my answer.

"Um, maybe. I'd have to ask my friends," I reply, looking around for my friends who are making their way towards the exit leading us back the way we came.

"Just....just don't leave tonight without seeing me first," Jase says as he grabs a hold of my hand. It starts to shake as he brings it up to his mouth and places a gentle kiss on the top of my knuckles. "Please. I want to see you again," he says with one last kiss on my knuckles.

I inhale quickly at the contact of his lips against my skin, eyes wide as I watch helplessly. I feel his warm breath fan against my hand and wonder what that breath would feel like fanning against my neck, my lips, and maybe even other places. *Holy crap! Down girl!*

"Okay," I finally say, struggling to get the

Lacey Black

words out over the lump in my throat.

He gives me a small smile. Not the cocky, arrogant smile that you see in the magazines or on television. But another of those sincere, happy smiles. This smile makes my stomach do a swan dive and start the backstroke.

He finally releases my hand and slowly backs away towards the door, the same way he entered to room. Our eyes remained locked until the last possible second before he exits the room entirely, leaving me yearning and longing for his return.

"Wow. You just had some sort of crazy moment with Jase Bentley," Avery says behind me.

"Seriously. That was hot. I was waiting for your clothes to magically fall off while observing that," Josselyn adds with a smile.

"Definitely. You were having hot eye sex, and now I feel like I need a cigarette just from watching," Erin says with a giggle.

I turn towards my girls and give them a dramatic eye roll. We all link arms and head back out into the arena to find our seats. Our seats are front row, dead center. When I leave tonight, I'm giving Maddox Jackson a huge kiss. Seriously,

36

these seats are amazing. Everyone is on their feet, standing and cheering as the lights go dark. Through the minimal lighting on the stage, you see the boots of the band members walking onto the platform, taking their designated places within the stage. The crowd around me is deafeningly loud. Josselyn is jumping up and down, screaming her beautiful little head off next to me. I can't help but look down at our tightly gripped hands. Her excitement and energy and that of the entire arena around us courses through my fully charged body.

The lights suddenly flash. Smoke rises from the depths of the stage. Bursts of fire shoot from the cannons. Drumsticks countdown the beat. Guitars strum the first few notes of their first single, "Fire".

And, finally, Jase Bentley walks on stage.

Chapter Four

Jase

I could do without the smoke and the fire, though I understand the significance of it, especially since our lead song is "Fire." I walk up to the microphone, center stage, and grab the guitar hanging from my neck. I scan the crowd quickly but with the blinding beams of the spotlights, I can't see past the first few rows. But, I do see the most beautiful pair of hazel eyes staring wide-eyed back at me from the middle of that front row. The screaming fans, the blinding lights, the music around me fades away until it's just us. Me and her. Holly. Hell, I don't even know her last name, but I will. By the end of the night, I will know her last name, her phone number, and so much more.

I belt out the lyrics I've known by heart since I wrote them eight years ago. I sing the words that are like second skin to me, singing for her and only her. I keep my eyes locked on hers as I belt out the words, line by line. My fingers strum my guitar completely on their own. Hell, they know exactly what to do.

"I'll burn it down, I'll bring you down, down to the ground, until you feel my flames, my burning desire, and you and I will be on fire."

The crowd goes wild, singing along with each word that pours from my mouth. But I'm completely lost in one particular mouth. I watch helplessly as I'm pulled into the depths of those hazel eyes, her delicious mouth moving as she sings along. She knows the words. Hell, everyone in the country knows the words to this song, but watching her sing these words is like I'm hearing this song for the first time.

The dramatic chords fill the arena as the song nears the ending. My eyes still glued on the only eyes I want to see as I sing, *"You do this to me, your touch is my desire. There's no way to save me, I'm burnt by your fire."*

The lights fade as the electric guitar and the drums finish out the final few notes of the song. The crowd goes wild, eagerly anticipating what song is next. All I want to do is finish this show so I can get backstage. Back to Holly.

We play a few more of our hit songs before I finally step up to the microphone and acknowledge the crowd. "Evening," I say as the spotlight drowns me in light. "Everyone havin' a good time?" I ask and throw them my trademark smirk. The crowd erupts in another ear piercing cheer. "Glad to hear. You know, we're excited to be here tonight in St. Charles, Missouri." Again, the crowd goes wild at the acknowledgement of their hometown. "And I have a special friend in the audience tonight who is celebrating her birthday. So, this next song is for Avery and her friends who are together celebrating tonight." I wink down at the ladies in the front row. Their eyes are all round with shock, mouths hanging open with surprise and excitement. Holly looks absolutely fucking adorable as she stares back at me from the front row. I have a few things I'd like to do to that sexy little mouth of hers. Hell, what I'd do to her mouth is only the beginning. But, right now, I have a show to continue and a few more songs to sing so I just grin down at her like an idiot and pray that she can't read my dirty mind.

An hour later, we step off the stage after a quick wave to the crowd and prepare ourselves for the encore. I grab the towel and wipe off my sweaty face, turning to scan the small crowd backstage for Phillip. When I finally spot him with his hand resting on the hip of some too-young woman with her fake tits in his face, I quickly make my way to him.

"Hey, I need a favor," I say as Phillip turns

his attention from the cleavage to me.

"Hey! Great show, man. I'd love for you to meet Monica," he says with a big toothy smile. Monica steps forward away from Phillip's hand and slides her fake boobs against my chest.

"Hi, there," she purrs as she winds her arms around my neck.

"Yeah, hi. Listen, Phil -" I start but am cut off.

"I hope it's okay if I keep you company tonight," she coos so sickly sweet I think I have a cavity.

Unfortunately for her, I don't have time for her brand of shit. "Not now," I grind out through gritted teeth. "Phil, those four girls who were backstage with us before the show, I need you to go get them. Bring them backstage after the show."

"Four girls?" Phillip laughs. "You dog, you!"

It's such a stupid comment that it doesn't even warrant a response. The guys are heading back onstage for the encore. "Don't let them leave, Phil. I mean it. Bring them backstage to me," I say as I disengage myself from the blond tramp rubbing against me like a cat in heat and turn to

41

walk back onstage.

"But what about Monica here?" Phillip hollers behind me.

"Entertain her yourself," I throw over my shoulder without even a backwards glance.

I step back onstage to start our three song encore, hoping that Phillip does his damn job and brings Holly and her friends backstage following the show. My eyes seek her out completely on their own as if she's a target and my eyes are heat seeking missiles. I find her right where I left her, smiling and laughing with her friends. She looks so carefree and happy. I envy her. What I wouldn't give to feel like the old Jase again. Let go of the inner demons that taunt me; the ghosts that haunt me.

I'm just finishing up the final song when I catch movement of a security guard heading towards her. Good.

Now to just finish my job, smile for a few photos, and head backstage to meet up with Holly. It's strange, you know? I've known her for five minutes, but it feels like I've known her a lifetime already. I feel different when I'm around her.

Like I can be myself.

Free.

Chapter Five

Holly

Some big burly mammoth of a man pushes his way through the throngs of people down the brightly lit hallway and into the large backroom. There are a handful of people milling around, drinking beers or whatever hard liquor fills their plastic cups. I scan the room but don't see any sign of Jase or the rest of the band.

"What are we doing here?" I ask quietly to myself.

"Well, I think we were summoned by the God of Rock," Avery says with a sassy smile. "Relax. You're acting like you've never talked to a boy before."

"Boy? Yes. Rock God? No. This is crazy, Avery. What could he possibly want to talk with us about anyway? It's not like we would have anything in common. He's him, and I'm me," I mumble under my breath, not really wanting to draw attention to myself. The women back here are beautiful with long, bare legs and perfect hair. They probably spend more money in one trip to the salon than I make in a week at the hospital.

"Don't be silly, Holly."

"But, we probably need to get back. You and Joss have babies at home waiting for you." Excuses, yes, I know. I've got more in my back pocket ready to fly on a whim.

"I just got a text from Maddox a few minutes ago and the kids are sleeping. Everything is fine so stop trying to conjure up some silly excuse to leave," Avery replies.

"But, -" I start, but am cut off by the feisty blond in front of me.

"No buts. Jase freaking Bentley invited you - us - to come backstage and hang out for a little bit. So pull up your big girl panties and suck it up," she demands sternly. "Wait, you're wearing cute underwear, aren't you?"

I sigh and roll my eyes at my best friend. "Of course I'm wearing cute panties. I was considering going over to Paul's after the concert."

"Paul's? Why?" Avery asks as she grabs a bottle of water from the large tub filled with drinks and ice.

"Well, if you must know, we've been seeing each other for a few weeks and I know he's been anxious to get horizontal. I thought maybe tonight I'd stop by and surprise him," I say in a quiet voice as I watch Josselyn and Erin retrieve drinks from the tub and continue their wedding talk.

"There's a reason you haven't gotten horizontal with him yet, Holly. Don't waste your time on him. It'll probably be bad anyway. You know, like 'file your nails or mentally make your shopping list' bad," Avery says between swigs of water.

"You're probably right," I start to reply when my spidey-sense starts to tingle. Well, more like my girly parts start to tingle. I swear I can sense his presence before I even catch sight of him, but I just know. Jase is in the room.

"Ladies, thanks for coming back and hanging out for a bit," Jase says from behind. The hairs on the back of my neck stand up and my body is instantly covered with goose bumps from the sheer closeness of his body and the deep timber of his voice. His voice sounds like sex. Again with the tingly girly parts.

"Hey, thanks for inviting us back here," Avery says.

"Yeah, I've never been backstage before," Erin adds.

"Do you ladies need anything to drink?" Jase offers as he reaches in the tub and pulls out a bottle of water.

Since I'm the only one without a drink, Jase hands me a bottle of water before reaching back inside and pulling another out for himself. He takes long, gulping pulls from the bottle. I watch his Adam's apple bob up and down with each swallow. I instantly want to step forward and run my tongue up that neck, tracing the long column of smooth skin with my tongue, maybe even sucking on that Adam's apple. *Get a fucking grip!*

"So," Jase starts as he leads me towards a quiet corner of the room. I check over my shoulder and see Avery, Erin, and Josselyn all talking to the rest of the band members who just blew through the door. "How'd you like the show?"

"It was amazing. When you wished Avery a happy birthday on stage, I think you could have pushed any one of us over with a feather," I reply.

Jase laughs that deep, throaty laugh. It's a great laugh. I'd love to hear it again, and again, and again. "Yeah, you all seemed a little surprised," he says before taking a long pull from the water bottle. Damn, I've never wanted to be a water bottle so bad in my life. "So, do you have a last name, Holly?" he asks with hopeful, sparkling eyes. Damn, those eyes are amazing.

"I do actually have a last name," I reply, fighting with everything I have to keep from smiling.

Jase stares back at me, huge grin splits across his devastatingly handsome face. "Are you going to share it with me?"

"Oh, you want to know what it is? I thought you just wanted to know if I had one," I tease.

"Sassy. I like it," he says with that promising grin.

"It's Jenkins."

"Holly Jenkins," he says as if trying it on for size. "So, Holly Jenkins, I know you're not married or engaged. Is there someone else I need to worry about?"

"Why?" I ask incredulously. No way is this rock star asking if I'm seeing anyone. Not possible. I wear minimal make-up and sometimes hate brushing my hair. I'm average, a size six. Not a toothpick with big fake boobs or a modeling contract. I love chocolate chip cookies and hot fudge milkshakes, for the love of God, and sometimes consume them for my supper.

Jase leans in, completely invading my personal space, and I'm instantly assaulted with his scent. It's all woodsy and sweaty and sexy as hell. His green eyes sparkle with seriousness as he says, "Because I need to know how many guys I have to get out of my way."

"Out of your way for what?" I whisper, completely lost in the sea of green eyes.

He leans in further, so close I can feel his breath fan against my lips. "Out of my way until I have you all to myself," he replies, his lips mere millimeters away from my own. I pray he kisses me.

NO you don't!

"I'm seeing someone," I whisper as I stare at those lush, lickable lips. Lips that promise to deliver so much more than a few lines of a song.

"Someone?"

"Yes."

"Name?"

"Uhhhh, Paul?" I stumble on the words, shaking my head as if trying to strengthen the connection between my lips and my brain. Why isn't my brain working?

"Was that a question?"

"No. His name is Paul," I finally get out.

"Paul, huh? Well, I hope you're not too attached to ol' Paul, Holly Jenkins. Because Paul doesn't stand a chance anymore," he tells me confidently. Those words coming from any other man would appear cocky and arrogant – everything I've accused Jase of being. But those words right now coming from Jase Bentley seem more like a promise. I shiver at the thought.

"What do you mean? Why wouldn't Paul stand a chance?" I defend, crossing my arms at my chest in a defensive stance.

Jase's eyes drop to the cleavage I basically just offered up on a golden platter with my little temper tantrum. He ogles unapologetically for a few moments before returning his eyes back to mine. "Well, Paul doesn't stand a chance because of me. You can pretend you're into this guy all you want. Go on forced dates, maybe give him an awkward, uncomfortable kiss good night. But I promise you, honey, in the end it's going to be you and me. I'm not saying that to be conceited. It's a fact. I feel it deep down in my bones. I know it like I know my own name or the words to every song I've ever written." His eyes are fierce and determined, and for some reason, I can't help but believe everything he's saying. Which is completely cray cray because he's him and I'm...well, me. And our worlds don't mesh.

I stare back into those deep green eyes and fight the urge to lean forward, just a few inches, and taste those lips that just spoke the most intense, intoxicating words I've ever heard. I feel his gaze down to my core. My lady parts are alive once again and doing a hula dance.

"Give me your phone," he tells me as he reaches his hand forward.

"Why?"

"Why do you ask so many questions?" he asks with a lopsided grin.

"Because." I say as I dig my phone out of my back pocket and hand it to him. Jase tries to wake up the phone, but it is password protected. One dark eyebrow rises up as he hands it back to me.

"Password?"

"You're so bossy," I reply with an eye roll and a smile. I take the phone, type in my four digit code, and hand it back to him.

Jase clicks on the camera and pulls me against him. He's like a brick wall. His chest is hard and unforgiving. I inhale a sharp breath as electricity pulses through my entire body just from the sheer closeness of this man.

"But, I already have a picture with the band," I tell him as I look up at him just over my right shoulder.

"True, you do. But, this one is just for you and me, honey. Now smile that beautiful smile for me," he says as he positions the phone in front of us, lining up the two person selfie.

The smile I give him is easy, natural. We both smile at the camera, our bodies pressed tightly against each other, his front to my back. It's comfortable. Genuine.

One quick flick of his finger and the photo is snapped and saved to my photo album. Jase gets to work with his long, lean fingers and before I know it, he hands me back my phone.

"What did you do?" I ask as I stare down at my phone.

"I sent myself that photo and added my contact information to your phone. So now you have no reason to not contact me," he adds casually.

"What makes you think I'm going to contact you?" I question.

"My gut tells me that you and I have only just started, Holly Jenkins," Jase says with a beautifully cocky smile. His eyes twinkle and his entire face lights up. I almost forget that he's a Grammy award winning artist. Almost.

"Hey, Holly. Jake and Maddox are about to send out the National Guard and the Air Force. We should probably head back to Rivers Edge," Avery says from behind me.

I turn towards my best friend, her all-knowing eyes sparkling with mischief. "We don't want Mr. Protective and Mr. Overprotective to send out the cavalry."

"Which one's which?" Jase asks with a chuckle.

"Could go either way. They are two men struck from the same mold and fiercely protective of their women," I tell him with a smile.

"Sounds like my kind of men," Jase replies.

Avery grins from ear to ear as she links her arm within mine. "Ready?" she asks.

"Yep," I reply and give Jase one last glance. I'm not ready to go. Not even close.

"One minute," he says to Avery with a wink as he pulls me out of her grasp and away from prying eyes and perked up ears.

"It was a pleasure meeting you, Holly Jenkins," Jase says with a slightest rise of the corner of his lip as he extends his hand towards me.

"You, too, Jase Bentley," I reply as I take the proffered hand. It's big, warm, slightly calloused from playing guitar, and feels oh so right wrapped firmly around my hand. I instantly want to feel those hands on other parts of my body.

And then before I have any time to process it, Jase leans forward and places a feather light kiss on my cheek. I revel in the warmth and the firmness of his lips. My eyes flutter closed completely on their own as I bask in the sensations flooding my instantly too hot and aroused body. I hear him inhale against my ear and all of the blood in my body rushes south. Before I can act on this overwhelming need coursing through my body, Jase pulls away and stands directly in front of me.

"Good night, Holly."

"Good night, Jase," I manage to mumble as I struggle to get the words out of my parched throat.

Avery links her arm back through mine, and we walk towards Erin and Josselyn who are waiting for us at the front of the room. The room is filling up quickly with girls flaunting their stuff and guys eagerly taking them in. When we get to the exit, I look back over my shoulder one more time, sure that Jase has already moved on to one of the half-dressed floozies running around the room. But, when I turn around, I find deep green eyes staring at me, watching me go. His face is serious, as if he's deep in thought. He catches my eyes and gives me a quick smile before I'm half pulled, half dragged out of the room. Away from Jase. Into the cold April night. Into the waiting limo. Back to Rivers Edge. Back to my solitary condo.

Back to real life.

Chapter Six

Jase

I make it maybe fifteen more minutes before I'm sneaking out of the big room and heading out to my tour bus. I'm supposed to be mingling with the VIP's and sucking up to the corporate sponsors, but my mind isn't in it tonight. Hell, my mind hasn't been in it for quite some time. But right now, my mind is lost in a beautiful pair of hazel eyes. Sexy, curly brown hair that begs for my hands to dive in and tangle those luscious curls around my calloused fingers. An enticing, sassy mouth that is begging to be kissed.

I step outside into the cooler April night and head straight for my bus. The fence line is still full of fans, mostly women, screaming my name; begging for me to invite them inside the bus with me. Not tonight. Not ever again. There's only one person I want to invite on this bus, and she's driving further and further away from me as we speak.

I throw the fans a wave as I step up onto my bus. My driver, Tom, gives me a polite nod but maintains his position in the driver's seat. I

55

head to the back bedroom and grab my phone off the small chest of drawers screwed to the wall. I scroll through the new text messages that I've received over the last four hours or so until I find the one I'm looking for. I bring up the photo that I sent myself from Holly's phone and stare at her beautiful, smiling face. I've met thousands of women, dated dozens of starlets, actresses and supermodels. None hold a candle to this woman. I save the photo into my phone, setting it as my background photo, and recall the words I said to Phillip when he asked me who she was. *My future wife.* Damn right.

I've spent a total of thirty minutes with this woman but she makes me feel more than I ever have. I feel alive. Like I've received my first drink of water after days in the desert. I feel like I could walk on water. I feel like I can finally live the life I want to have. The life *I* want, not the life everyone around me tells me I want. She makes me feel all of these things. It's exciting, sure, but it honestly scares the shit out of me, too.

Before I can talk myself out of it, I text a quick message.

Home yet?

It doesn't take but a few minutes before my phone pings with a reply.

Halfway there

I flop down on my bed, my home away from home three hundred nights a year, settling in for another message.

Who's driving?

Bill. Limo driver. ;-)

Front row concert tickets, backstage passes, AND a limo?

Yep, she's a lucky woman.

So, where's home?

Rivers Edge 30 minutes away

And so we text and text. The next thing I know it's forty-five minutes later and we've talked about her family - parents Bob and Lucy, older sister Jackie, and younger brother Aaron - her job as a nurse at the local hospital, and even touched on a few of her hobbies. I've answered a few of her questions about myself, but haven't delved too deep into myself yet. That's a whole kettle of fish for another night.

I should probably let you get to sleep. I hit send on my phone as I gather up a change of clothes for the shower.

I'm going to jump in the shower before bed. Wash this rock concert off of me ☺

Well, if that doesn't put dirty images in my mind, nothing will. Shit. I would give all of the money in my bank account to join her in the shower right now. To wash her body from head to toe.

Me too. Too bad we aren't together. We could share a shower ;)

I start to wonder if I went too far when my phone dings again.

Too bad. Maybe next time ;)

Hell-fuckin-yeah! At least I know this attraction isn't one-sided. Hell, I already knew it wasn't one-sided despite what she said about seeing some guy. I could see it in her eyes and written all over her face when I kissed her on the cheek. She wanted more. Hell, if I wasn't in a room filled with people, I would have given it to her.

I settle for a quick, *Good night, Holly.*

She replies instantly. *Good night, Jase.*

I drop my phone down on the bed and grab the cotton shorts from the dresser. The bathroom is pretty small in my bus and consists of a small sink, toilet, and shower stall. I turn the water on scalding hot. I always jump in and let the burn wash away all the sweat, grime, and perfume that's stuck to my skin. No, not because I was hooking up with someone, but because these women throw themselves on me, hang on me, grind and paw all over me every night.

I'll be a lying ass if I didn't say that at first this lifestyle was fucking awesome. Women everywhere. Willing women. Lots and lots of women. Now, just the thought makes me ill. I don't want that lifestyle anymore.

As the hot water scalds my already overheated body, I can't help but lean my forearms against the cool shower stall wall and close my eyes. The water rinses away the sweat, but doesn't touch the images forming in my mind. Holly naked in the shower. Holly running her soapy hands up my wet chest, caressing my neck with her nimble fingers, placing gentle kisses against my stubble-covered jaw. I'm rock hard at the dirty images parading through my mind on repeat like some late night porno. I try to fight the desire coursing through my body like an out of control freight train, but I can't. It's impossible. I want her too much.

I take a hold of my engorged cock and start to pump like a teenager. I should be embarrassed at a little self-love in my shower in my tour bus, but I'm not. I keep my eyes closed as I imagine her face, her smile, her laugh. I imagine it's her hand wound tightly around me, followed by her sweet mouth. Her tongue licks up and down the length of me just moments before she wraps those lush lips around me and gently sucks me deep. I imagine the moans and the sounds she makes as she gives me oral pleasure. Her sweet moans as her eyes remain locked on my eyes are what finally push me over the edge. I shake and gasp for air as I unload myself in the small confines of the steamy shower stall.

I don't want to open my eyes. I want to imagine that she's right here with me, right now at this moment, running her tongue over every inch of my still pulsing cock. I shudder once again as I release myself and grab the soap to finish my shower. When I open my eyes, reality sets in and I'm all alone with my thoughts.

I'm just starting to step out of the stall and reaching for my towel when I hear Phillip's loud voice from the other side of my bedroom door. I barely have time to wrap the towel around myself before there's a quick double knock and my door flies open.

"What are you doing in here? We have sponsors that were expecting to hang with you, Jase. You can't just run off. This is part of the job, and you know it," Phillip chides as he takes in my towel clad body. "Are you coming back inside?"

"Nope. I'm done with people tonight," I tell him as I slip on my running shorts.

"Jase, these people come from all over to see you. You need to remember who really pays your bills, man."

"I get that, Phil. Really, I do," I state as I snatch a clean t-shirt from the dresser. "I'm serious when I tell you, I'm done. I'm tired. I want a life. I want to settle down somewhere and maybe someday give the whole wife and kid thing a try," I say as I slide the shirt over my still-wet head.

I look up at Phillip when I don't get a reply. He's looking at me with a horrified look on his face. "You're fucking serious?"

"As a heart attack."

"Is this because of Camille? Or that girl you met tonight? What was her name?"

"Holly. And no it isn't about either of them. I've been thinking about this for awhile. When this leg of the tour is done, I'm taking a break. I'm taking time off. I'm thinking a year to start with, maybe more."

"Jase, come on, man. You're not thinking clearly. This is what you do, who you are. You are

Jase fucking Bentley. You take time off and you'll never be where you are right now again. You are at the top now, man. You'll be lucky to play small college stadiums and state fairs," Phillip says with a look on his face. It's one of pure horror and shock.

"Well, maybe that's what I want. Maybe I want to play those little places again." I take a seat on the bed and look up at him. "Maybe I'm ready to step back and let the next big act take my place in the limelight. I'm not saying I want to quit completely. I just need a break. We've been going non-stop for more than three years now. I spend holidays on the road, stuck in a tiny tour bus or a hotel room. I'm rarely at my house in LA anymore. I have to schedule phone calls with my family and friends. I'm just ready to step back and relax a little." I plead with him to understand with my eyes.

Phillip runs his hand over his face and through his hair causing it to stand up a little. "I see what you're saying, Jase. Are you sure? I mean, really, really sure?"

"Yeah. I'm sure."

Phillip exhales dramatically as he sits down next to me on the bed. "Okay. I'll talk to the powers that be. We won't extend the tour after this leg. Two more months. Can you get through two more months? Because I need you in this. We have deals and sponsors and we can't start pissing these people off, Jase. This business is too damn small to start pissing everyone off. You'll never get another deal."

"I understand. And I appreciate your understanding, too."

"Well, I can't say I completely understand, but I get it. We won't be breaking any contracts if we finish this thing out. Then, you take some time and screw your head back on straight. When you're ready, we'll get right back in this thing."

"*If* and when I'm ready to come back, you'll be my first call," I tell Phillip honestly.

"Good to hear," he replies with a small smile. Phillip quickly stands up and walks towards the door. "I'm going to head back in there and smooth over the ruffled feathers. I'll tell 'em you're not feeling well or something. We should be ready to pull out of here by two a.m."

"Sounds good. Hey, Phillip?" I say as I stand in front of my friend, my right hand man. I hold out my hand as I say, "Thank you."

Phillip looks down at my offered hand and takes it firmly inside of his. "You're welcome,

Jase. And thank you for taking me on this ride with you." He gives me a cocky smile. "It's been one hell of a fucking ride."

I laugh and pat him on the shoulder. "It sure has."

"Don't forget we have that interview with Trace Donohue Monday in Chicago. Then we have the media tour starting in Indianapolis and winding our way towards New York. Friday morning we have the hospital tour thingy, and then two nights in New York City and Boston. You'll be busy over the next several weeks, man, but it isn't anything you're not used to."

He's right. I am completely used to this, but it still doesn't make it any easier. After Phillip leaves the bus, I lie back on the bed and flip on the television. I had a satellite installed on the bus when I bought it so I can pretty much get whatever I want whenever I want it. I settle on a movie channel showing a Jason Bourne movie and wonder what Holly's doing. I'm sure she's sleeping now that it's after one a.m.

Two months. I can surely finish this thing on top and finally get a little peace and quiet, right?

Chapter Seven

Holly

On Monday morning, I'm walking down the corridor after eating a burger in the cafeteria, heading to the emergency room when my phone buzzes in my pocket. I dig in the big pocket on the front of my scrub top and see a text message from Jase. When I open it, he has taken a selfie picture of himself with the Willis Tower in the background. His headline reads, *In Chicago. You?*

I step into the first available empty room and pull the curtain to give myself a little privacy. We're not supposed to have our cell phones while on duty or in the emergency room with us, but most of us do. As long as we keep it on vibrate and in our pocket, they usually don't say too much.

I snap a quick selfie with the blue and green striped curtain in the background and fire it back. *Working,* I tell him.

It doesn't take long before he replies. *You look beautiful.*

Okay, I'm not going to lie. I blush. A lot.

I just fire back, *Why thank you* ☺, when the curtain behind me flings open. Paul is standing there with a big smile on his face. My gut tightens as the smugness on his pretty-boy face. I drop my phone back in my pocket before he can ask any questions.

"Good morning. I've been looking for you," he says as he reaches forward, grabbing my hip and pulling me forward. I stumble a little and fall into him.

"Hi, Paul. What's up?" I say as I pull back and out of his arms.

"Oh, I've been having a morning. Dr. Tomlin is such an idiot. I've been following him around, cleaning up his messes all day. He actually told me to back off once or he'd have me removed from the ER!"

"Well, he is the doctor, Paul."

"Yes, but I know what I'm doing. I have almost as much schooling as he does and more experience."

Okay, this man is completely full of crap. First off, there is no way that Paul - a RN - has as much school as Dr. Tomlin unless he failed nursing school several times. Plus, Doc T is in his fifties. I think he holds the trump card on experience.

I'm practically held hostage by his constant rambling and complaining for the next five minutes. I started tuning him out though around ten seconds into his rant, and my mind drifts to Jase. Heck, my mind hasn't stopped thinking about Jase. I thought about him long after we stopped texting last night. I dreamed about him. And I've walked around in some sort of love-sick puppy dog trance all morning. I can't seem to get him out of my head. It's like he's pitched a tent and taken up residence.

"So, you see what I'm saying, right? You know that the man is just completely impossible to work with. Anyway. Dinner tonight? I was hoping we could spend some time together. Alone. If you know what I mean," he says as he wiggles his eyebrows at me and I feel my gut take another twisting dive straight to Nauseaville.

What did I ever see in this man? He's impossible and needy. He's everything Avery told me he was - cocky and arrogant. Yes, the package may be wrapped up nicely, but inside, it's nothing to write home about. "Sorry, Paul. That's not going to work. In fact, this isn't really working for me. I'm just hoping we can go back to being friendly colleagues again," I tell him, determined to cut this man completely from my life once and for all.

"Seriously? But we didn't even sleep together yet. Ask all the other nurses. You don't know what you're missing, baby," he says as he strokes his thumb against my cheek.

I shudder, and not in the good way. I pull back, repulsed that he touched me and so thankful that all I ever did with this man was share a few kisses and maybe get a little handsy.

"Yeah, that's okay, Paul. I'm good," I tell him as I step back several steps and head towards the door. "I'll see you around, okay?"

I don't even wait for an answer before I turn and hightail it out of that room. I can't get far enough away from him. Did he seriously think I was going to reconsider my break-up just because we hadn't slept together yet? Actually, the more I think about it, that doesn't surprise me as much as it should have.

I can't wait to tell Avery.

*****

After work, I stopped by the grocery store

for food. Cabinets and fridge - all empty. It was either buy food or lick the cheese out of the stale Ritz sandwich crackers in the cabinet. I opted for real food. Following an extended run through the aisles of the grocery store, I finally make it home from work, two hours after my shift ended. I'm starving so I quickly throw a chicken breast in the skillet and cut up some fresh broccoli for the steamer.

I don't eat healthy all the time, believe me. I crave sweets and sugar like nobody's business, but I do try to keep my meals simple and on the healthy side when I can. As I'm pulling the chicken from the stovetop, my phone pings with a text alert. I retrieve my phone from my purse and can't help the schoolgirl excitement that takes over when I see Jase's name on the screen. I slide my finger over the screen and stare at his incredibly handsome face. He's standing in front of a colorful backdrop with big block text. The headline underneath the picture says, *Trace Donohue Show in 30 minutes.*

I snap a quick picture of myself with a smile and a thumbs-up and tell him to, *Break a leg!*

Just as I'm about to set my phone down, he texts back.

I'll call you after taping.

Ok, I respond quickly.

I'm staring at my phone with a silly grin on my face when it hits me square in the gut like an ex showing up on your wedding day. Camille Douglas. Why the hell is Jase Bentley talking to me when he has a beautiful, supermodel girlfriend waiting at home for him? Is he really that kind of guy? Does Jase get off on finding small town, regular girls and showering them with a little attention, all just to what? Sleep with them? Of course he is.

My stomach flips and the nausea sets in. My chicken is forgotten as I sink onto the couch. Why is Jase Bentley calling me? I can run different scenarios through my head until I'm blue in the face, but there's only one person who can answer that question. When he calls - *IF* he calls – you can bet your ass I'm going to find out!

Avery calls for our regular chat at six – okay, six-fifteen. She's always late.

"I need out of this house! Please tell me that you can go for a walk with me tonight," she says as soon as I answer the phone.

"Sure. What's going on?"

"Oh, Ryder has been fussy all day and I

need a breather. Maddox is giving me an hour to get away. Can you meet me at the entrance of the park?" she asks.

"Sure. Give me five minutes to change out of my scrubs and throw on sweats. I'll be there in a few minutes," I tell my best friend.

"Great. See you there," she replies before signing off.

I throw on my comfy black yoga pants, an old sweatshirt, and my favorite Nikes, grab my keys and head out the door. A few minutes later, I'm pulling in and parking next to Maddox's truck. She hops out and you can see the tension radiating off of her.

"What's wrong?" I ask, concerned for my best friend.

"I just need a break. Ryder isn't sleeping well yet and had a rough day. Brooklyn is giving me guilt trips for not playing with her as much as I used to, and Maddox is walking around with a constant hard on because, and I quote, 'these four weeks are the longest of his entire life.' Seriously, you'd think he's never gone more than a few days without sex before. I know he went months and months when he was in the military. It's not like there were a lot of options overseas," she adds when we hit the brightly lit walking path through the local park. There are several other people on the path tonight, all taking advantage of the mild April evening.

I can't help the chuckle that comes from my throat. "I wish I had some magic answers for you, Ave, but I don't. When can you have sex again?"

"Well, it's supposed to be six weeks, but I'm about to give in tonight. Not only is Maddox grumpy and horny, but I'm about ready to burst myself. Every time he takes off his uniform, my body practically orgasms on its own just by watching him. It's taking all the self-control I have not to jump him. I can't wait two more weeks," she says deadpanned.

"You need to just rip off your clothes and parade around naked. You know that man can't resist you when you're naked. Do you want me to watch the kids so you guys can have some alone time?" I offer.

"Tempting. Let me see how tonight goes and then we'll see," Avery says. "Oh, before I forget to tell you, Mom cornered me in the kitchen last night at family dinner and wanted to talk."

Avery's family gathers every Sunday night at her parent's house for dinner. I go whenever I can which isn't nearly as often as I would like.

Her mom's cooking is absolutely outstanding. I have to unbutton my pants just to get in my car to drive home afterwards.

"Mom is taking me on as a partner at the bakery," she says as her entire face lights up with excitement.

"Really? I didn't think she would be ready to retire for awhile."

"Well, she has been thinking about it more now that she has three grandkids. She wants to watch them for us. I guess Amber is already talking about quitting and going back to school, so her thought is to bring me in and we'll do it together for a few months while she shows me the ropes. We'll hire another person to replace Amber later in the summer, and when I'm ready she'll turn it over to me completely," Avery says with a huge smile.

"That's amazing! I know this is something you've wanted for awhile," I reply as we continue walking down the path.

"I have. Maddox and I talked and if she's ready, then I'm ready. I grew up working at that bakery, and now I imagine showing Brooklyn the ins and outs of that place, baking cakes and cookies."

"Who are you going to hire to replace Amber?" I ask.

"I'm not sure. Maybe we'll put an ad in the paper?"

"Well, I'll keep my ears open for you," I add.

"Okay, good. So, what's going on with the rock god?" she asks with that cat-that-caught-the-canary smile.

I sigh dramatically as I stare ahead at the path in front of us. "I don't know, Ave. Honestly. We texted for awhile after the limo dropped me off Saturday night, all day Sunday, and a few times today. He told me he's in Chicago to do the Trace Donohue Show and is going to call me afterwards," I tell her.

"That's good, right?"

"Ave, do you remember that he has a girlfriend? He's dating one of the most well-known supermodels in America. The one on last year's cover of the swimsuit issue of *Sports Illustrated*. It was only a few weeks ago that his picture was plastered all over *People Magazine* with her at that fundraiser for that big, new children's hospital. I can't - No, I won't get involved with a cheater. I will never be the other woman."

"Have you asked him about this? I mean, I, of all people, understand where you're coming from here. If he's just going to use you for a little fun on the side, I'm going to cut off his nuts and mail them back to him in a Ziploc baggie."

"Ouch. Yeah, if he's just playing around, I'm pretty sure I'm going to cut off his nuts, Ave," I add with a laugh.

"Well, I think that before you lose any sleep over this or give yourself anxiety, you should just ask him what his deal is."

"I plan to. He's supposed to call me tonight, so I'm going to ask him outright then," I say as we round the last curve that leads us back to the parking lot.

We're both quiet for a few minutes as we make our way back towards our vehicles. I'm sure Avery is taking advantage of the uninterrupted quiet, and my mind keeps moving ahead to the upcoming phone call with Jase. Will he admit to cheating on Camille?

"Thank you so much for walking with me. I needed some time with my bestie," Avery says as she leans in and wraps her arms around me for a fierce hug.

"Anytime," I tell her. "If you want me to come over one night so you can go on a date with Maddox, just call. I'm happy to come over and snuggle with my kiddos."

"I just may take you up on that very soon," Avery replies. "Actually, what do you think of a sleepover with Brooklyn? I think she could use a little Aunt Holly attention."

"Deal. Let's set it up someone soon."

"She will be so excited. And maybe Maddox and I can take advantage of a little alone time once Ryder goes to sleep," she says with a wishful smile and a wink.

Avery throws a wave at me as she climbs into the truck and backs out of the parking lot. I climb quickly in my car and head towards home. When I get the key in the lock of my front door, I hear my phone ringing. I was in such a hurry to get out of the house and walk with Avery that I forgot my cell phone on the counter with my purse.

"Hello?" I say as I answer the phone.

"Hey. It's Jase. I've been calling for about twenty minutes. Is everything alright?"

"Yeah, it's fine. Avery called and wanted to go for a walk. I didn't take my phone with me,"

I reply.

"How was the walk?"

"Good. Beautiful night for it," I reply as I get comfy on the couch.

"So, how was work today?"

"Um, good."

It's quiet for a few moments. I don't really know the best way to ask the question I need to ask, so I decide to just jump in with both feet. "Look, Jase. I need to ask you something," I begin.

"Shoot," he replies.

"What about Camille?" I finally spit out breathlessly. I sit back, legs tucked protectively against my chest as I hold my breath waiting for his response.

"Camille? What about her? We broke up," he says so matter-of-factly.

"Well, I haven't heard anything about a break-up, Jase. Your entire life is splashed all over the television and the internet. I can't help but wonder what you're doing calling me."

Jase sighs and I hear a door shutting in the background, drowning out the noise of the street around him. "I broke up with Camille well over a week ago. I honestly don't know how it's been kept from the news this long. The only thing I can think of is that she's waiting for me to come crawling back. Not happening."

"So you're not seeing her anymore?" I ask and again, hold my breath while I wait for his answer.

He doesn't hesitate. "No. Absolutely not. It was actually long overdue. I'm not dating Camille or anyone else for that matter. See, my problem is that I can't stop thinking about this woman I met a couple of days ago. I think about her while I'm traveling in my bus. I dream about her when I'm sleeping. I even fantasize about her while I'm in the shower," he admits which makes my blood pump and my body hum with awareness. My mouth goes as dry as the Sahara Desert.

"You do?" I whisper, suddenly my brain can't seem to function properly and form words.

"Oh, yeah. She has these amazing hazel eyes that suck me in and hold me hostage and this perfect little mouth that I long to kiss. I imagine her long, slender legs wrapped around my waist, preferably with nothing between us. I picture the noises she makes while I kiss up her neck to her ear. I can't wait to explore her body from head to toe. I yearn to learn what makes her tick, what makes her wild."

I clear my throat and will the words to come out, but I got nothing which is so not like me. He has completely thrown me off guard. My entire body is on fire, and I feel completely hypnotized from his intoxicating words. I can almost feel his mouth on my neck as he talks about it. "That's a very lucky girl," I finally spit out, breathlessly.

"No, that's the thing. I'm the lucky one."

"So, this girl. When are you going to see her to tell her all of this?" I ask, his word-porn melting me into a big pile of hormonal mush.

"As soon as possible. See, the thing is that I'm on the road, committed to this tour for two more months. As soon as I'm done, I'm going to find this girl and show her everything I want to do to her," he whispers into the phone in that low, sexy voice that I crave to hear. "I'm going to do all of the things I've been imagining doing to her for two long, lonely nights. I'm going to tell her all about the things I'm doing to her and how I feel about her."

"Wow," I say and clear my throat again.

"So, how was work today?" he asks casually, switching gears so fast that I almost have whiplash, while my entire body is flush and overheated.

"Umm, it was good. I broke up with Paul today," I tell Jase.

"That's the best thing I've heard all day, babe. So, let me get this straight. You're single. And I'm single. Right?"

"That's the way I understand it," I reply with a smile.

"Sounds like you and I have a few things in common. I have your phone number and you have mine. So, maybe we call and text each other and see what happens."

"I think I can handle that," I say.

"And I think that you'll be the only woman I call or text while I call or text you," he says and I can't fight the huge grin on my face.

"I think that's a solid idea. I won't call or text anyone else either," I reply.

"Good to know, babe. Listen the buses are getting ready to pull out. We're heading to Indy tonight for a radio tour and then we're weaving our way up the East coast towards New York. I'll call you or text you every chance I get, okay?"

"Okay," I respond. Again, that stupid

schoolgirl smile is plastered on my face.

"Sweet dreams, Holly," Jase practically purrs into the phone like liquid sex.

"Good night, Jase," I reply as we both hang up.

I set the phone down and just stare at the blank screen. Oh, I am so in trouble. I am so far out of my league with Jase that I don't even know which end is up. There are too many unknowns in this whole relationship. I know we just started talking, but it already feels like a relationship. He is so different than any other guy I've dated. Will my heart even survive the devastation and destruction he would leave behind in his wake after it's over? Can I, Holly Jenkins, RN, actually have a relationship with someone like Jase Bentley?

The only thing I do know for sure is that I'm willing to find out.

Chapter Eight

Jase

My cell phone rings in the front pocket of my jeans, and I can't help the excitement that courses through my body at the thought of Holly calling me. I know I just talked to her last night, but the idea of hearing her sweet voice on the other end of the line has me tied in knots. I step away from the guys as I pull the phone from my pocket. Shit. Camille. I hit the silent button before sliding the phone back in my pocket.

I just get back to the guys who are chatting with a few executives at WROC radio when my phone rings again. I don't even pull it completely out of my pocket this time. I slide the tab to silent and return it again to my pocket.

Jesse, my bass guitarist, gives me a questioning look with a raised pierced eyebrow. I shake my head and return my attention to the two men and woman in front of us. Twice now, Deidre has slid up next to me, touching my arm or my back in a suggestive way. Maybe a few years ago, hell, probably even several months ago, I would have found her subtle flirting attractive and considered enjoying her company for a bit, but not now. The thought of spending any time with anyone other than Holly turns my stomach.

We finish the tour of WROC, Deidre making her way through the small group and resting her hand again on my forearm.

"So, what do you think of our studio? You can see why we're dominating the ratings here in Indy and the surrounding areas," Deidre says with a sparkling smile. She's a very attractive woman with her sandy blonde hair and green eyes.

"You have an impressive set up here. And we're glad you play Bent's hits as strongly as you do in your rotation," I tell her matter-of-factly.

Deidre runs her hand up my arm and leans in a little, her mouth very close to my ear, rubbing her ample breasts against my bicep. "You know, I would love to take you out for lunch after the tour is over."

"Ah, well I appreciate the offer," I start as I slowly pull back as to not draw too much attention to the fact that I'm pulling away. "We're actually heading out in just a few minutes and have to be on the road heading to our next stop."

"But you have a few minutes? I'd love to have a quick chat with you in my office," she offers. I've been around this block many, *many* times and know that there won't be much chatting if I accompany her into her office right now. Unless you count her saying my name over and over again as chatting.

"Again, I appreciate the offer, but I'm not interested," I tell her as I completely disengage myself from her.

"Huh," she huffs. "I thought all rock stars look for that golden opportunity for a little no-strings sex," she says quietly with her arms firmly crossed over her chest.

"Most do. I'm seeing someone though, and I don't think she'd appreciate me *chatting* with you in your office or anywhere. And honestly, I'm just not interested. No offense to you, Deidre, but I just don't think it's a good idea."

She laughs. *Laughs*. "Puleeeze! You've slept with half of the country. Plus, I know you're not seeing anyone. You're all over the news as of about an hour ago, reports stating that you and Camille broke up," she huffs.

"True, we did. I'm not talking about her. It was nice to meet you, Deidre, but it's time for us to head out," I tell her as I start to turn towards Jesse and the rest of the band.

"You'll stray. Men like you aren't capable of monogamous relationships, Jase. It's how you're built," she spits out before turning and rejoining the two men who lead our tour.

I walk towards the exit, posing for a bunch of pictures and signing a few autographs for fans that have gathered just outside of the studios. I shouldn't be bothered by her words – hell, I don't know her from Adam – but, for some reason, I am. She knows nothing about me, yet her words strike me straight to the core. I'm done being the man I was in the past. I want to be a better man for myself *AND* for a woman in my life. Holly? Fuck, I hope so. I've known her days and talked to her mere hours, but the thought of having her in my life – for the rest of my life – settles me. Calm washes over me, setting down the turmoil that's buried inside of me, slowly eating me alive.

We've been on the road for a little over an hour, going over our schedule for the next few days when I remember that my phone is on vibrate. The thought of Holly trying to call me and missing the call enters my mine, leaving me anxious, so I pull out the phone and turn back on the ringer. I have seventeen missed calls and voicemails and thirty-six text messages. I excuse myself from the table and cue up the voicemails, hoping that something isn't wrong with my parents or one of my brothers.

"Hey, darling. I really need to speak with you about this little media thing. I have a great idea on how we can spin this so-called breakup. Call me back. I'll be waiting."

Delete. Next. "Darling, I'm not sure why you won't answer my phone calls, but I need to talk to you. The media is outside of my condo and want to know why we broke up. Call me."

Delete. Delete. Delete. Delete. "Darling. This is getting out of hand. Where the hell are you? We did not break up!" she seethes into the phone.

Fuck. Not surprisingly, the rest of the messages are the same basic message but Camille gets more hostile with each one. By the time I get to the seventeenth message, every other word out of her mouth is profanity. I pace my bedroom as I try to decide what to do about Camille. I scan through the text messages. Most of them are from her, a few from my family asking about the break-up gossip on the news, and one from Holly. I ignore all of the other messages for this moment and tap on Holly's. It's a photo of her beautiful face snuggling up to a baby. I grin down at my phone like an idiot. She's wearing the biggest smile and the love and adoration is evident in the photo. The message says, *Snuggles with Ryder.*

I snap a quick pouty face selfie that I'm almost embarrassed to take a picture of and send. Almost. I type a quick message, *New man already?*

My phone signals to life a few minutes later.

Hardly. He's just my other man. ☺

Another man? I don't share well, babe.

Ryder is hardly competition, rock star. He's not much of a talker and I have to clean up after him. Plus I like my man a little taller.

Well, he is cute – I'll give him that. But he better keep his hands to himself!

I'll pass along your message as soon as he wakes up.

So, shit is hitting the fan. Camille is raising hell in the media. U hear?

Yeah. U ok?

I'm getting ready to talk to Phil on how to deal with it. I'm ok tho. Wish u were here.

Me too. I'll let u deal with Phil. TTYL?

Abso-fuckin-lutely, babe. Call ya later.

Bye

I type back quick messages to my parents and my brothers to let them know that Camille and I did, in fact, break up, that I was more than fine with it, and that I'd call them all later.

When I exit the room, Phil is pacing around the front of the bus with his phone pressed to his ear and the guys are all sitting around the couch and table talking. Well, they were talking until I walked out. Now they're all staring at me and the bus is eerily quiet.

"What?" I ask.

No one says anything for several seconds as they all exchange looks. Jesse finally stands up and approaches me, head slightly hung down and without making eye contact. Apparently, he drew the short straw.

"What?" I repeat with more edge in my voice. I look up at Phil who has stopped pacing and has turned to face me, his attention still on the phone in his hand.

"So, Camille has gone to the media now that word is out about your break-up," he starts and clears his throat and looks around like he's buying time. He sets his hand on my shoulder and gives it a little squeeze as he tries to soften the blow he's about to extend to me. "After the media found out this morning about the break-up, she's claiming that, that you…" Jesse takes a deep breath and I realize I'm holding mine. "She's claiming that you have anger issues."

"What? I don't have anger issues! Why would she say that?"

"First off, settle down, Jase. I know you don't have anger troubles, man, but freaking out isn't going to help you at all where the media is concerned. Phil is on the phone trying to track down her publicist and the source of the bullshit claims, but all he's found out so far is that she talked to a few paparazzi outside of her condo just a little bit ago. She had the waterworks going and everything, apparently," Jesse mumbles and gives me another shoulder squeeze.

Son-of-a-fucking-bitch! How can this be happening? I close and open my fists a few times trying to regain control of my emotions just as Phil yells something into the phone and slaps it down in the table.

"Well?" I ask anxiously.

"It's not good, Jase. Apparently, the media caught wind of your break-up this morning and started calling the label for confirmation. Before they could get with us after the radio station interview and tour this morning, Camille walked outside and told the media at her door that you guys broke up last week after she asked you for a break, you went nuts, and threatened her. She supposedly had to threaten you with a restraining order just to get you to leave her place after you tore it up."

"When did this supposedly happen? I've been on tour for the past three weeks," I seethe through gritted teeth. My jaw is so tight, it's painful.

"I'm working on getting the details. Obviously, since it didn't happen, there's no police report, Jase. It's her word against yours right now. But we definitely need to respond to these outrageous claims as soon as possible. I don't want to wait on this at all. We need to be aggressive and deal with this immediately before she has time to spew more hatred."

"What's this going to do to his reputation and to the band, Phil?" Jesse asks with concerned, yet venomous eyes.

"The way you guys - especially Jase - are in the media right now? It'll be ugly, guys. It's hard to gauge how bad, but with Jase being in the public eye the way he is, everyone will be talking. Even if we can prove she's lying, I'm afraid of the damage that will be done. Professionally and personally," Phil responds with direct eye contact.

"So, what next?" I choke out. The thought that I'm going to have to put myself in the direct spotlight sickens me. The media are going to pounce on me. Everything. My personal life. My family. My past. It's all going to become public and scrutinized in the worst way possible.

"My assistant is drafting a press release with Publicity right now. She'll email it within the next few minutes and we'll review it. Once we've both approved it, she'll send it out to the major news sources. Publicity is also working on lining up some appearances for tonight and tomorrow with a few major networks on the east coast. We'll get this squashed as quickly as possible, Jase."

Phillip's phone rings almost immediately after he finishes talking, and excuses himself to take the call. The guys all offer their encouragement, but I can see it in their eyes. They're worried about me, but also their careers. This is their livelihood, too. This band is their life as much as it is mine. Suddenly, my decision to step back from touring for awhile takes on a whole new light. It's not just me who is stepping away, I'm taking it all away from my band mates – my friends – too. Shit. Something I've never thought of before.

I excuse myself and step back into my

room. I fire off another text message to my parents and my brothers telling them what I'm sure they already know. That these latest accusations are false and just a desperate publicity stunt by a desperate woman.

Then I call the one person I'm actually scared to call. What's to keep Holly from tucking tail and running for the hills with these accusations? She doesn't really know me yet, and to her, this could be a deal breaker. Hell, I wouldn't blame her for running far, far away from me. Fuck.

I run my hand through my hair as I wait for her to pick up the phone. It rings five times before I hear her angelic voice.

"Hello?"

"Hey," I say, exhaling loudly. Holly is quiet for a second, causing my heartbeat to skip and my breathing to pick up pace. "So, I imagine you've already seen the latest?" I ask.

"Yeah. Avery and I were just watching The Toni Shaw Show and they did some sort of dramatic breaking news thing."

"It's not true, Holly. I know we just met and you really don't know me, but I would never do what she's accusing me of. I would never flip out like that to the point of destruction. I would never intimidate a woman like that."

"Why is she doing this?" Holly asks in a quiet voice.

"I have no clue, babe. Phil said she confirmed the break-up to the media and said I flipped out because of it. The truth is we broke up over the phone because I'm on tour. I haven't seen her in almost three weeks. The last time was when she flew into Tulsa and we met up at a show. She left the next day to head to St. Thomas for a photo shoot. I knew it was over before she even left Tulsa, but because of my schedule, I didn't get to talk to her and end it with her until last week. I swear on my mother's life that I never freaked out on her like that."

"I believe you, Jase. I know we just met and I don't really know you that well, but I just…I just feel like you are someone I can trust."

"You can trust me, babe. I promise. We're working on getting this shit taken care of. I can't ask you to stand by me while this shit-storm comes down on me. I wouldn't blame you for taking off and never speaking to me again. I just pray like hell that you don't. There's something about you. I need you. And if I'm being completely honest, that scares the shit out of me.

I've never depended on or needed anyone before, but the thought of not hearing your voice on the phone or seeing your beautiful face on my phone screen brings me to my knees. Holly, what the hell is happening to me?" I ask, sighing deeply, not able to camouflage the pure anguish in my voice.

"I don't know what's happening, Jase, but it's happening to me too. I think about you all day and dream about you all night. You consume me. And that scares me, too," she whispers.

"Fuck what I wouldn't give to hold you in my arms right now. I would give a year of my life just for a few moments of holding you," I tell her honestly.

"I'm not going anywhere, Jase. I'll be right here waiting for you," she tells me and its music to my damn ears.

"I promise I won't let you down, Holly. I'm going to get this taken care of and come for you. You know that, right? I'm coming for you and when I see you next, plan on being tied up for a while. Maybe even literally," I add with a chuckle.

Holly laughs and says, "Well, I can't wait to see you."

A knock sounds on the door and Phillip

pops his head in, indicating that he wants me in the main seating area of the bus. "Listen, babe, Phil needs me so I better go. I will talk to you later tonight, okay?"

"Definitely. Bye, Jase."

"Bye, babe," I tell her before hanging up. I drop my phone in my pocket and head out to hear the latest from Phillip.

"Okay, here is the press release," he says as he offers me a piece of paper. "We're lining up a few interviews still, but this release is about to go nationwide. We'll let everyone know that her accusations are fabricated and unwarranted, that you guys broke up via phone last week, and that you haven't seen her in three weeks."

"I had a phone full of text message and voicemails from her this morning. She was asking me what was going on and with each message she became more aggravated and hostile. By the last message, she's the one who completely flipped her fucking lid."

"Good, good. Don't do anything with those message," Phillip tells me.

"Well, I deleted most of them, Phil. After I started getting into them and she started to change her tune, I decided to save them. I have the last several. Plus, all the text messages."

"That should still be good. We're almost to Columbus, Ohio and we're there for the night. We'll arrange for the interview with the band first and then we'll talk about the accusations at the end of the interview."

"Sounds good," I reply, rubbing my forehead as if trying to fight off the headache forming. "If you don't need me anymore, I'm heading back to take a nap."

"Fine. I'll work on the questions for the press," Phillip replies as he turns and heads back to the front of the bus to the table he uses as his makeshift office.

Once back in my room, I flop down on my bed, stretching out my long body. My shoulders are tense and it feels good to stretch out, but relaxing isn't happening. Not right now. I contemplate calling Holly, again, just to hear her voice, but I don't want to bother her again so soon. I'll call her later. I opt to call the one woman who I can always talk about what's on my mind without judgment and criticism. I grab my phone and call my mom.

Chapter Nine

Holly

I'll be honest. Completely freaking honest. You ready? I am completely smitten with Jase Bentley. Not in a crazy fan-girl way, but in the crazy girlfriend way. We talk every night before he takes the stage and usually as soon as he can get away from the post-show festivities afterwards which tends to be very early in the morning. Every free moment I have at work, at home, in the car, wherever, I spend it with him. Via phone, of course. We've taken up SnapTalk this week, too. I never, ever would have thought I'd download that free app that all the teenagers use, but I definitely see the advantages of it lately.

It's been a month since the Camille scandal rocked Jase's life, but he's handling it well. The press is split with half of them crucifying him and buying into Camille's claims, wondering when he was going to enroll in anger management therapy, while the other half support him and are smearing Camille's not-so-good, lip gloss covered name.

Camille sticks by her claims and when

interviewed, even manages to turn on the waterworks as she recounts how scared she was and how she feared for her life during her rage-induced nightmare.

Jase did a handful of interviews both on television and on radio sticking to his side of the story. The one thing I've noticed though, his fans are still loyal. They still buy Bent tickets nightly. Concerts are still sold out and their music is flying off the shelves. America feeds off drama, doesn't it?

I try to ignore the magazine covers in the grocery store, but it's harder than I thought. Pictures of Jase and Camille from the past are plastered all over the cover of every major magazine and newspaper in America.

I find myself falling more and more for the man I've only seen in person for a very short period of time. He knows everything about me at this point, and I feel like I've gotten to know the real Jase. Not the man he portrays to the public. No. I see the sweet, gentle, loving man underneath his tattooed exterior. I hear his real life. I see his real smile. I know his true heart.

Tonight, I try to push all thoughts of Jase out of my mind. Tonight, I have a date. Not just any date, but dinner and a sleepover. Brooklyn will be here any minute for our one-on-one play date and sleepover. She's been a fabulous big sister to Ryder, but Avery has felt that she could use some Aunt Holly one-on-one time without her two month old brother in the spotlight. So, that's why I'm pulling out all the ingredients for Bean's favorite chocolate chip muffins on a Wednesday night. I don't have to work tomorrow and Bean doesn't have preschool. So, tonight we're having dinner wherever she wants, watching Grey's Anatomy on Tivo, and snuggling on the couch.

I hear Avery's vehicle pull in the driveway that I share with my neighbor a little after five. I hear the car doors open and close moments before my front door flies open and slams into the entryway wall. My favorite little blue eyed, blond haired five year old bounces into the room like she owns the place.

"Aunt Holly, I'm here," she exclaims from the entryway.

"And she may have taken off a chuck of your drywall," Avery hollers behind her daughter, stumbling in with an overnight bag and princess pillow.

"It's fine. I know this handy cop that I can call to fix things like that," I holler back from my kitchen.

Lacey Black

"What are we doing, Aunt Holly?" Bean asks cheerfully from the entryway of the kitchen.

"We are going to make chocolate chip muffins, sweetie," I say as Brooklyn jumps up and down with excitement.

"Really?! My favorite!" Brooklyn exclaims.

"Yes, really. Run in the bathroom and wash your hands, and we'll get to work," I tell her just seconds before she takes off down the short hallway.

"So, how's McHotty Rockstar?" Avery asks with a sly grin.

"It's a little weird that you call him that, you know?"

"It's not weird. It would be weird if I said it to his face," she replies.

"Yes, I imagine that would be weird...for you. He's probably used to it," I reply.

"So, how's it all going? I thought for sure that whole Camille debacle would die down by now, but the stupid story seems to keep plowing, full steam ahead."

"I know," I reply with a sigh. "Jase is acting like everything is okay, but I know it's

100

bothering him. I can tell in the tightness of his voice when he talks about it, even though he tries to smile and tell me everything is fine." I grab the hand towel and re-dry the counter tops so that I have something to do with my hands.

"When are you going to see him?" she asks.

"The tour has one more month, so I assume maybe then. He keeps saying that he's coming here as soon as he's done," I confide in my best friend.

"And that makes you feel...what?" she asks.

"Happy. Elated. Excited. Take your pick. I don't understand what's going on with us, Ave. We talk so much that I had to up my data plan on my cell phone because I was hitting my limits halfway through the month. I'm just nervous, you know? I have all of these crazy feelings swarming around inside, and I don't know what to do with them. Do you think this is rushed? Is this all too soon?"

"Too soon?" Avery asks with a chuckle. "I slept with Maddox on our first date. We were engaged two months later and married three months after that. I'm probably not the best person to tell you if this is all too soon or not," she says.

"Yeah, but you and Maddox were practically in love before you went on your first date. Everything else was bound to happen."

"Maybe, maybe not. The point is that only you and Jase can determine what is too soon and what isn't. If it feels right, then go for it. You guys are on the phone day and night and have been for four weeks. You guys are becoming friends before lovers. If and when that happens - and I better be your first call with all the dirty details - only you can determine what's next for you guys," she says.

I think about her words for several seconds before she adds, "What are you nervous about?"

I choose my words carefully as I say, "What if he gets here and realizes that I'm nothing special? What if he gets here and realizes he made a mistake in wanting to be with me?" I say quietly.

"Impossible. You are the best person I know, Holl. You are funny and passionate and have a great fashion sense. Why do you think I steal your clothes all the time? Jase Bentley already worships you, and when he gets here, he's not going to be able to let you go. I guarantee that great things are ahead for you and McHotty Rockstar," Avery says with a beautiful smile.

I walk around the kitchen table and pull my best friend into a fierce hug. "I love you," I whisper.

"I love you more," she says, returning my squeezes. "And besides, if he hurts you, I'll have Maddox and Jake arrest him for stupidity."

I laugh at the thought of Maddox and Jake taking pride in torturing Jase. Poor Jase.

It's just after eight o'clock, we're neck deep in McDreamy, and we've consumed a half dozen chocolate chip muffins when my phone pings from the end table next to me. I look down at Brooklyn and notice her eyes are starting to glaze over as she continues to munch on popcorn on the couch. It won't be long and she'll be out cold for the night. I grab my phone quickly and smile when I see Jase's name on the screen. It's a text message.

Whatcha doing?

Grey's with Bean. Girl's night .You? I type out my reply and hit send.

It takes him several minutes to reply, but when he does, he sends a photo. I click on it quickly and stare down at his smiling face. I smile back at my phone for several lovesick seconds before I take in his surroundings. Just over his right shoulder is my neighbor's bright blue fence across the street and over his left shoulder is my car.

As I slowly start to stand up, a knock sounds at the door. My heart stops. My mind blanks. My breath sucks in hard. Standing on the other side of my front door is Jase.

I release the lock, throw the deadbolt, and fling open the door. His smile could light a thousand homes with the wattage. He's wearing worn jeans that fit him oh so right, and his trademark black t-shirt. We both stare at each other with big, goofy grins on our faces for what feels like forever. Eventually, Jase steps forward and places his right hand on my hip. Heat inundates my body at his touch. My mind floods with vivid recollections of my late night fantasies starring Mr. Jase Bentley. And now, the fantasy is standing right in front of me. It's been thirty-two days, but he's actually standing here.

I step forward as he gently tugs my hip towards him. His body is hard as I move into his embrace, wrapping my arms firmly around his waist. His other arm snakes around my back as we revel in the feel of each other.

After several heartbeats, Jase pulls back and runs his hand down the side of my face. I'm lost in his emerald green eyes as my breath comes out more of a little pant. Talk about the best kind of surprise.

"What are you doing here?" I finally ask.

"I needed to see you. I couldn't stay away any longer," he replies as he continues to stroke my face, his pointer finger dipping down and caressing my bottom lip. His eyes drop down and he stares at his finger and my lips. You can see the internal struggle he's fighting as his eyes become stormy and intense.

Kiss me, I want to scream from the top of my lungs.

"I didn't want our first kiss to be in public where anyone can see," he whispers as he steps forward until he's mere inches from my face. He's losing the fight, I can tell, and I'm ready for him to concede.

"Aunt Holly? Who's here?" Brooklyn hollers from her place on my couch.

We both freeze, eyes wide, with the realization that we're really not alone.

"Who's that?" he asks with a slight raise of the corner of his mouth.

"That's my niece, Bean," I tell him. "I'll be right in, sweetie," I holler over my shoulder. "Do you want to come in?" I ask, hopeful.

"I didn't fly for two hours in my disguise, rent a car and drive for over an hour just to stand on your front porch," he replies with that devilish smile.

"What's your disguise?" I ask, again taking in the t-shirt that molds to his arms, his worn Levi's, and his black boots.

He reaches down and pulls a dirty red baseball cap out of the side pocket on his duffle bag. He places it on his head, adjusting it until it sits low, covering his eyes.

"That's your master disguise? My five year old niece could pick you out anywhere," I tell him with an ornery smile.

"I didn't say it was a good disguise," he adds, feigning hurt, with a gentle flick of my nose.

"We better step inside before my neighbors start snapping pictures and selling them to the tabloids," I tease and turn back towards my condo.

"Who dat?" Brooklyn says from the couch, pointing at Jase.

"This is my friend, Jase. He stopped by for a visit," I tell her before turning towards Jase.

"Is he having a sleepover, too?" Brooklyn asks with big, innocent eyes.

"Uh, we'll see," I tell her as Jase smiles down at me with that wolfish grin.

"I was, in fact, hoping for a sleepover," Jase whisper under his breath. "But I see that you already have company tonight," he adds and glances back at the blond on my couch.

"Brooklyn and I were just watching some Grey's. Why don't you join us?"

"I don't want to impose. I can grab a hotel room," Jase says.

"I can guarantee that if you do that, word will spread faster than the California wildfires that you are in town. You can't go to the hotel, Jase," I tell him. "You can camp out on my couch."

"Your couch? Alone? I haven't had to sleep on a couch in years, Holly," Jase says with a cocky smile and a raised eyebrow.

"And if you had any luck at all, I wouldn't already have a bedmate tonight. Unfortunately for you, you're a little too late, Jase," I reply just as sassy.

"Your sass is turning me on," he replies deadpanned which causes me to laugh.

"Come on, let's watch Grey's." I throw an elbow into his hard six-pack abs, causing a dramatic exhale of air on his part. Jase throws his duffle bag on the floor next to the couch and plops down next to me.

Brooklyn is snuggled up to my right side as Jase extends his arm over the top of the couch and his legs straight out in front of him on my left. I can't help the schoolgirl glances I give out of the corner of my eye. He's so damn hot. And he's here.

After my third or fourth glance, Jase catches me. Or I catch him looking at me - either way. The corner of his lip curls up as his thumb begins to rub gentle circles along the back of my neck. Jase moves his hand completely underneath my hair and caresses the skin on the back of my neck with his palm. His hand is hot. Jase. Is. Hot. This is when I audibly sigh.

"How long do you have your houseguest?" Jase asks, nodding towards Brooklyn. I glance down and notice Brooklyn's eyes closed as she drifts to sleep on my lap.

"I'm meeting Avery for lunch tomorrow," I tell him as I absently smooth her hair away from her face.

"And then what?" he asks.

"What do you mean?"

"Do you have to work?"

"Not until Friday morning at six," I confirm, sucked into the depth of his striking green eyes.

"So, you have no plans after lunch tomorrow until six a.m. on Friday?" he asks, still stroking my neck.

"None," I reply.

"Well, I just happen to be here - in Rivers Edge - until Friday morning at five a.m." Jase leans in until we're practically nose to nose. I try not to move so that I don't wake Brooklyn, but the urge to eliminate that air between us is great. I lean in until our lips are a breath apart. "So, the way I see it, we have about seventeen hours to get to know each other in person instead of on the phone. Seventeen hours to figure out where this is going."

"Where do you think it is going?" I ask, breathlessly.

"All the way, baby. I can't explain it, but I feel drawn to you like I've never felt before. Like a moth to a flame. Like a singer to a microphone. I feel alive and free when I'm talking to you; like I can be myself for the first time in forever. And I'm trying my damnedest to not scare you off right now, but I feel all kinds of crazy ass things when I think of you. Things that I've never felt or never wanted to feel, and as much as I'm trying to not scare you, I'm terrified on the inside because what I want from you is forever," he whispers against my lips without actually touching them. His words are his caress.

"You know that after a few weeks of talking on the phone?" I ask, eyes wide with shock.

"I knew it from the moment I saw you standing at that Meet and Greet, Holly," he says. I watch as he closes his eyes, takes a deep breath, and pulls back. "But, I'm not going to rush you. First, I need to take you on a date," he adds with a smile.

"A date?"

"Yep. Tomorrow night. You'll have to pick the place since I'm not familiar with your town...yet," he adds confidently.

"Awfully confident there, aren't we?" I ask, trying to fight off the smile that is threatening to take over my face.

"Definitely, confident. I'm just getting started with you, Holly Jenkins. That's a promise," he says with those emerald green eyes boring into my soul. At this exact moment, I know he's being one hundred percent honest with me.

And I know that I want him to be one hundred percent right.

Chapter Ten

Jase

Holly's couch fucking sucks. Period.

I've been tossing and turning on this little thing for the better part of two hours. It wasn't made to sleep a six foot man comfortably. Around two a.m. I turned on the TV and muted it just so I could try to distract myself. The problem is the brunette sleeping on the other side of the closed door is more of the distraction. I wonder which side of the bed Holly prefers. I itch to run my hand along the side of her face while she dreams. I long to feel her smaller body pressed firmly against mine.

I finally sit up and turn the volume on low. This is the time I'm usually winding down each night, so when Holly decided to take Brooklyn to bed around nine-thirty and stay in there with her, I know I was in for a long night. That didn't stop us from texting each other from a room apart. I smile as I watch late night reruns and think about our bantering back and forth. Her head on her pillow in the next room; my head on the throw pillow on the couch – just me and my hard on.

And to top it off, I have yet to steal my first real kiss.

I scrub my hands over my tired face. Damn I have it bad.

I grab my phone and type out the quick text before I can even think. *I can't stop thinking about you.*

There. Sent.

Pussy.

I set the phone down quickly and grab the remote, searching for anything other than *Seinfeld*. My phone buzzes a second later so I grab it, smiling at the name on the screen.

I'm having the same problem ☺

My fingers type. *What are you thinking about?* Send.

Our date, she sends back a few seconds later.

What about it?

I think we should go to the Mexican Restaurant in town. Less people.

I will take you wherever you want to go as long as you're there with me.

It takes her a few minutes to reply, but

when she does, I'm not prepared for her honesty. *I'm scared at how fast I'm developing feelings for you, Jase.*

I suck in a jaded breath of air. *I'm fucking terrified, too. But the thought of not having you in my life is more terrifying. I don't know what all this means yet, but I want to find out.*

I do too, she texts. It's music to my damn ears. It's a beautiful melody that I can't get out of my head. Holly wants to give this a go as much as I do.

Sleep, beautiful ☺

Yes, sir ;)

I set my phone down and lay back on the couch, trying to get comfortable, but knowing that Holly is literally on the other side of a wooden door and *not* halfway around the country is doing crazy things to my heart. It's beating wild in my chest. I long to touch her, smell her hair, and taste her lips.

I toss and turn for the next thirty minutes, lost in the images of Holly sleeping feet away from me.

Welcome to the longest night of my life. Sleep isn't an option anymore.

*****

I decide to go to lunch with Holly, Avery, and Brooklyn. Donning my red baseball cap, we walk into the café and find a corner booth open. Holly and Brooklyn slide in, me on the outside with my back to the rest of the café, as we wait for Avery.

"She's always late," Holly says with a smile as she passes around menus.

"Yeah, Mommy is always late," Brooklyn chimes in. "Daddy says it makes her daring," she adds.

Holly and I both laugh. "Do you mean endearing?" Holly asks with a smile.

"Yeah, that," Brooklyn says and looks over her menu. Can she even read it?

"I want pancakes," Brooklyn says with a big smile. "And chocolate milk!"

"You had pancakes and chocolate milk for breakfast," Holly says, shaking her head.

"Yeah but I want them again," Brooklyn says, turning her big blue doe-eyes towards me and Holly. Holy hell, I wasn't prepared for that look. Yeah, that kid could have whatever the hell she wants.

"Fine," Holly says with a grin.

The waitress arrives at that moment, staring down at me. I drop my head down a little as if browsing the menu further while Holly orders drinks for her and Brooklyn.

"And you, sir?" the waitress asks.

I don't even glance up as I reply, "Coke, please."

The waitress lingers a few extra seconds before turning and heading behind the counter to get our drinks.

"I think she has your number," Holly whispers as she peruses the menu.

"Yeah," I mumble as I keep my head down.

"I don't know how, though. With that stellar disguise, I don't know how your own mother could pick you out of a crowd," she adds lightheartedly.

I can't help the laugh that erupts from my gut. Half the diner turns and looks our way. I don't look over my shoulder at them to confirm their suspicions, but I know that my time to be incognito has probably expired. I reach up and remove the hat, tossing it down on the seat between me and Holly.

"Better?" I ask her with a smile.

"Much," she says with her own smile.

Just then, Avery comes barreling into the café and slides into the seat opposite me. "Sorry I'm late. I was heading -" but Avery stops dead in her tracks, staring across the booth at me and Holly.

"Mommy, this is Jase. He sings songs," Brooklyn says so matter-of-factly that you can't help but laugh.

"Yes, Brooklyn," Avery says as she leans down and kisses the top of Brooklyn's head. "Jase does sing songs," she adds without removing her shocked eyes from me.

"Are you just going to stare the entire lunch hour, Ave? If so, it's probably going to get a little awkward in here," Holly says with a sassy smile.

"Oh. My. Gosh. What are you doing here?" she asks, shock still evident on her pretty face.

"I stopped by for a visit," I tell her, dropping my head back down as the waitress returns with our drinks.

"Are you guys ready to order?" she asks. I can feel her eyes burning into me.

"Yes, Bean wants the pancakes with whip cream and I'll take the BLT sandwich with sweet potato fries," Holly says.

I look up and indicate for Avery to go next who orders a quarter pound cheeseburger with everything and cole slaw. Finally, the waitress returns her eyes to me. "I'll have the roast beef with cheddar cheese and sweet potato fries," I tell her as I close my menu.

As soon as she finishes writing my order, she reaches for the menus around the table and says, "Do I know you?"

"I don't think so," I say, returning my eyes to Holly.

"You just look so familiar, though," the waitress says. She's in her late twenties with brown hair pulled back in a tight ponytail and hazel eyes. She's definitely cute, but not Holly.

"This is actually my first trip to town," I tell her.

It's always comical when you see that moment when they realize who I am. Her entire face lights up with a combination of shock and excitement. "Oh my God, you're Jase Bentley!"

she exclaims loud enough to draw attention from everyone in a two block radius.

"No, that's not me," I tell her. "I get that all the time, though," I add, shaking my head.

"Really? You look just like him," she says, but the look on her face says that she doesn't believe me. Her eyes squint closed a little as she takes me in, up and down.

"Yeah, if I was *the* Jase Bentley, do you think I would be in Rivers Edge, Missouri right now?" I ask.

"Well, that's probably true," she says, still eyeing me up and down. "I'll go get your order in." As soon as the waitress is out of earshot, Avery and Holly both turn their full attention to me with smiles.

"How often does that happen?" Avery asks.

"Honestly? Everywhere I go. There's no escaping it. And it won't be long before she realizes I was lying to her. They always find out," I tell them.

"Don't look now, but I think she's already figured it out, Jase," Holly says.

I look over my shoulder just as the waitress is taking pictures from behind the counter with her cell phone. "And those will be online in about four point two seconds," I reply with a shake of my head.

I turn my attention back to Holly and link my fingers with hers on the bench.

"So what are you guys doing tonight?" Avery asks with a sly grin.

Oh, do I have ideas of what we'll be doing tonight.

"We're going to dinner at El Toro," Holly says as she looks down at our linked fingers.

"Thursday nights aren't as busy so you shouldn't have too many people staring at you the entire time," Avery says while Brooklyn colors a picture on the back of her white paper placemat.

The waitress returns with our lunches, and we all dive in. I almost have my meal consumed when the first fan approaches our table. She's a young girl, probably about sixteen, and she has the biggest smile on her face. She tells me she's eating lunch with her mom before heading back to school, so I sign her notebook. Soon, the next fan comes up and asks for a quick autograph. And so it continues for the next twenty minutes.

Avery and Brooklyn get ready to take off, putting jackets on as they slide out of the booth. I stand up and extend my hand to help Holly from the booth. Her skin feels warm and soft against mine. Tingles of awareness course through my blood as she stands before me. I grab her hoodie jacket and help her slide it on.

Avery approaches Holly. "Thanks for spending time with Bean last night and today," she says as she pulls Holly into a tight hug. "And don't forget to wear pretty panties," she adds in a whisper which is still loud enough that I can hear.

Holly whispers something back to her that I don't hear and turns back to me.

"Ready?" I ask as I link our fingers back together.

"Yep," she says.

We follow them out the door and approach my rental car. Holly quickly removes the booster seat and hands it to Avery.

"I know you're here for only a short visit, but next time you can stay longer, we'll have you guys over for supper. Maddox is dying to meet Coy's little brother," Avery says with a polite smile.

"Deal. I believe I'll definitely be back soon," I say to Avery, but keep my eyes locked on Holly's hazel ones.

Holly rewards me with her beautiful smile. The one that causes her eyes and nose to crinkle up just a little. I don't even hear what Avery and Brooklyn say as they walk away. I'm lost in that smile. Those eyes.

"Let's head back to your place," I tell her as I open the passenger door for her.

But before I can let her slip down into the soft leather seat, I pull her flush against me and kiss her. I didn't want our first official kiss to be on the side of a street in broad daylight where anyone and their cousin could see, but I needed this kiss. I've wanted, dreamed about, and fantasized about this kiss for so long, it felt like the only thing I could do in the moment was take it.

Her lips are warm as my slightly rougher ones caress against her. My entire body goes fucking haywire as I become alive – really alive - for the first time in forever. My hands pull her tightly against me as I devour her sweet mouth. She tastes like coke and French fries and I'll be damned if it isn't the biggest fucking turn on ever. This is so much more than the body's natural need for release.

I feel her mouth open slightly and I take the opportunity to slide my tongue inside. Her tongue lashes against mine hard and swift causing every drop of blood I possess to rush south of my waist. Holy hell, this woman kisses like a fucking dream. A wet dream.

My hands glide up her body and into her curls. Her hair smells like something sweet and clean. I tighten my hands, fingers locked within those sexy curls, as I continue to kiss her intoxicating mouth. How long do we kiss? I have no clue. But when reality finally starts to snake its way into my lust filled mind, I realize I need to pull back. Pull back or take this somewhere more private.

"Let's get out of here," I say as Holly's labored breathing fans out across my chin.

"Okay," she whispers, barely audible.

I slowly pull back, but Holly's grip on the back of my shirt keeps me from going anywhere. I give her a sly grin until she realizes she's death gripping my shirt. Her cheeks turn the cutest shade of pink as she drops her hands and clears her throat.

I say nothing as I turn her towards the open door and help her inside. I walk around the hood of the car and give myself that old forgotten pep talk. The one where I tell myself to slow down or I'll scare the girl off. I haven't had to use that talk since high school which causes me to smile like a goofball as I reach my car door.

I'm so damn excited for our date tonight that I don't even notice the cameras. I don't even notice the crowd that had gathered, lurking in the distance, snapping pictures as if their life depended on it.

I don't notice until it's too late.

Chapter Eleven

Holly

I'm almost ready in the bedroom when there's a knock on my door. "You about ready?" Jase says through the door.

"Yep," I reply as I squirt my neck with my favorite perfume. I give myself a quick once over before heading towards the closed door.

I throw it open and am totally amazed at the man before me. Jase is every bit of the Rock God: he is in dark jeans and a crisp black button up shirt with the sleeves rolled up to his astonishing tattoo covered forearms. He scream pure sexy appeal. His hair is dried from his shower, but has that wild, unkempt look to it. It reminds me of sex.

"You look amazing," Jase says as his eyes roam from my soft curls to my black V-neck sweater and down to my skinny jeans and black kitten heeled boots.

"You're not so bad yourself," I reply as I step out of my room and into the hallway.

"You ready? I've been starving for those steak enchiladas since you mentioned them earlier," Jase says as we head towards my front door.

It's early May and the nights still have coolness to them. The trees are returning to their lush, green state and the birds are singing again. We step outside and head towards Jase's rental parked behind my car in the driveway. Once we're both belted inside the car, Jase drives us to El Toro on Main Street.

I love this place. The walls are bright and the décor is authentic. The Mexican flag hangs on one wall as do several pictures taken in Mexico by the owner on one of his early trips back to his home country.

"This place is great," Jase says as he sits in his chair opposite me.

"I love it here. The food is amazing," I say before I take a sip of the water our waiter just set in front of us.

I notice a few of the other patrons glance in our direction, but no one seems to make a big deal about the man in front of me. After we both order the steak enchiladas, refried beans, and Spanish rice, we fall back into that same comfortable talk we've had since I met him a month ago.

"So, can I ask you something?" I ask.

"Absolutely," Jase says before taking a bite of the homemade chips and salsa.

"Well, I might have read up on you recently, and I wanted to ask you about something I read," I say as casually as possible.

Jase raises his eyebrow as he waits for me to ask.

"In one interview, they asked you why you never write love ballads. You didn't really answer the question so I was wondering why."

He sits there for a few moments and takes a drink from his beer. I start to think he's not going to answer my question when he finally does. "I guess I've just always felt that if I was going to write a love ballad, I should be in love to do it. Or at least have been in love to understand it, you know?" he says without looking up from the chips and salsa.

"You've never been in love?" I ask, finding it very hard to believe.

"Have you?" he asks, his beautiful green eyes finding mine for the first time since we began this conversation.

"Yes," I tell him. "It was young love, but love no less."

Jase's face takes on a fierce and slightly pained look as he grips the edge of the table. He stares at me for several minutes before finally leaning in and saying, "The thought of another man being before me makes me want to rip this table apart."

I'm stunned silent by his words. I continue to stare at him as the sheer honesty of his words seep into my brain. The thought of a man - any man - having this kind of caveman type of reaction to me is thrilling.

The waiter delivers our food right about that time which is a godsend because I seriously couldn't figure out how to respond to what he said.

Jase takes a bite of his dinner before he continues, "So, to answer your question, no, I have never written my own love ballad. The few Bent has recorded were written by other members of the band or we purchased them. Someday, I hope to change that and finally write my own song," he says with serious, soul-deep searching eyes.

"I hope you're able to write your own someday, too," I finally say.

The rest of dinner is pleasant. I don't think I've ever laughed so hard during a first date, even though Jase and I have known each other for several weeks. Technically, it's still our first date. I also don't believe I've ever felt comfortable enough to truly be myself on a first date. I can't help my sarcastic side that presents itself when I'm with Jase, and fortunately, I don't think it bothers him too much. In fact, it seems like it turns him on more when I'm sassy.

The air in the car on the ride back to my house is electrically charged. The need and want is evident in his eyes as he continues to glance at me while he drives us back to my condo. Jase continues to stroke my knuckles as our linked fingers lie on his leg. It's comfortable. Exciting.

When we pull into the shared driveway of my condo, Jase parks behind my car. He shuts off the ignition and turns to face me. His green eyes seem to be more intense, glowing as they are illuminated by the only light coming from the streetlight outside.

Jase slowly brings my hand up to his lips. His lush, full lips continue to work over my knuckles just as his fingertip had. My breathing is shallow as I watch him caress my skin. I want those lips on mine more than I want anything right now. I long to feel those lips on other parts of my suddenly very hot body.

The air is sucked out of the car like some sort of vacuum as Jase slowly leans in. I lick my lips without even realizing it until Jase's eyes flair with need as they train on my lips and my tongue.

This kiss is as electric as it was earlier. The only difference is now, we don't have to stop. Now, we can go inside and see what comes after the kiss. And, God, do I want to see what comes after the kiss.

After several minutes of tasting my lips, Jase pulls away and exits the car. I see him adjust himself as he comes around to help open my car door. It's a heady feeling to know exactly what kind of reaction I give him.

Without saying a word, Jase leads me towards the front door. My hands have a slight tremor to them as I insert the key into the lock and give it a turn. Jase reaches over and turns me so that I'm facing him. His hands run from my jaw up and into my hair. His mouth descends on my jaw as he runs open mouthed kisses up the same path as one of his hands. His mouth lingers for several moments on my earlobe causing me to go weak in the knees.

As I start to sag against him, Jase pulls me

hard against his body. His body is a-freaking-mazing. Seriously! I will never tease Avery again about her drop dead gorgeous husband because if I never get to see another man as perfect as Jase again, I would still die a happy girl. Jase is perfection.

His lips are firm and he tastes delicious. He's all spicy from dinner with a hint of the beer he consumed. But more than that, he's hot as he kisses me like I've never been kissed before. He makes me feel like there's never been another kiss before this one.

"Come inside," I whisper as Jase's mouth nips at the skin behind my ear. Holy Shit!

Jase says nothing as he turns us both towards the open door and pulls me inside. Inside and towards my bedroom. Towards the moment I've been waiting for all night. Heck, all damn month. Maybe even my entire life.

Chapter Twelve

Jase

To say I'm nervous is an understatement. I've slept with supermodels, actresses, and debutants with too much money, but for some reason, the thought of finally getting naked with Holly has me shaking in my black boots.

I stare straight into her beautiful face. Her eyes are dilated and her breathing is still labored from the kiss. I don't want to just rush her back to her bedroom, but I'm damn close to giving in to the craving. And that's what she is. She's a craving. She's a drug. She's my hit.

I touch the soft skin of her cheek, caressing it while I gaze into her eyes. "I want to take you to your room right now, Holly. I want to shut that door, lock us away from the world, and do all of the things I've been fantasizing about for a month. If that's not what you want, tell me now. I'll kiss you goodnight right here in the living room and go to sleep on the couch. I'll get up in the morning and we can continue to get to know each other via phone and text. If you don't want to take this to the next step, I'm okay with that. It won't scare me away or make me run. I just -" I get cut off as Holly's sweet lips press firmly against mine.

"I want to go to my bedroom. Right now. With you," she whispers against my lips.

My blood flares to life as I scoop her up in my arms. She doesn't have to tell me twice. I want this more than she'll ever know.

In three strides, I'm rounding the corner and heading into Holly's bedroom, her body tucked securely in my arms. I don't stop until I'm lying her down on the bed. Her lips attack mine before I have the chance to pull away.

She licks my lips as my hands dip under her black sweater. One touch of her stomach, the skin all soft and warm, has my blood boiling. My entire body is like a lit fuse, ready to blow. I savor the feel of her skin as I slowly make my way up to her tits. My fingers graze over lace as my mouth continues to consume her. I'm a man possessed.

A moan rips from Holly's throat as my hand grips her lace-covered tit. My mouth waters at the prospect of tasting them. I tear my mouth away from hers and stare down at her. Her hair is fanned out on the top of her comforter and her eyes are dilated so that I can't even tell their color. Her breathing is coming out in quick little pants.

I look down, squatting next to her on the bed. I focus all of my attention on the thin sliver of bare skin peeking out between her sweater and her jeans. I use both hands to slowly slide her sweater up until her marvelous chest is revealed. Holly is wearing a black lace bra and her nipples are strained against the tight, sexy material. My hands twitch and my cock jerks against my zipper.

I can't fight it any longer. My mouth descends on her a fraction of a second later. Her nipples are hard little nubs as I suck them through the lace and into my mouth. Her moan is like music to my ears. The best kind of music.

Holly's hands snake into my hair, holding me firmly against her heaving chest. Once I show plenty of attention to the first little pebble, I move on to the other. I squeeze and massage her tits as she withers underneath me. My cock is painfully hard, begging to be released from its denim prison.

Once I've showered her chest with plenty of attention, I slowly kiss down her stomach. She sucks in air as I tickle my way down to the button of her jeans. With a quick flick of my fingers, her jeans are unsnapped. I look up one more time to gauge her response as I get ready to remove her pants.

Her eyes are wild and lust filled. Her

slightly open mouth is sucking in air like she hasn't had a full breath in days. I see the trust in her eyes as I rake mine over her beautiful face.

I slowly unzip her jeans and start to remove them. Black lace peeks out at me as I slowly pull down her pants. Torture. That's what this woman is doing to me, but it's the best damn torture I've ever experienced.

When I finally get the jeans down past her thighs, the picture of Holly wearing black lace boy cut underwear greets me from the bed. The material is snug and wet at the apex of her legs. My mouth goes dry and my heart tries to do a fucking tap dance out of my chest.

Once I get the jeans the rest of the way off, followed by her socks, I return my attention to that little slip of wet material. I slide my hands up her smooth, soft thighs as I slowly separate them. The scent of her arousal assaults me. I'm a drowning man, and she's my last gulp of air. I need her that much.

My hands find that black lace and slowly begin to stroke her through the material. Her moan is intense and fuels my already burning fire within. I can't stop myself as I slide the material to the side, exposing her core for the first time. This moment is better than any fantasy I've ever had about her. This moment is real. This moment is forever.

I bend down and run my tongue along her seam. She shudders and gasps under my touch. I waste no time as I pull her legs up, bending them at the knees and position myself between them. As I continue to lick and suck at her core, her legs wrap around my neck. Talk about a fucking turn on. I could explode right now in my pants.

I use first one, then a second finger, and explore her. She's warm and tight as I get to know her body. Her legs tighten around my neck as I bring my tongue back to the pulsing nub at her center. With a few hard flicks of my tongue as I continue to work her over with my fingers, she's gasping for air and moaning her release. Her entire body is shaking, her insides gripping my fingers in the best way possible.

After her body lays limp and sated on the bedspread, I finally glance back up at her. Her eyes are closed and her lips hold a slight, happy smile. Her arms are extended over her head which causes my body to practically spasm with excitement. I've had so many fucking fantasies about tying her up like that.

"I'm not done with you yet," I tell her as I hover over her. Her scent and taste are on my mouth as I devour her lips in another fiery kiss. My hands are everywhere. Removing her sweater and bra. Running up and down the length of her torso. In her hair. Holly wraps her legs around my waist, and I wish at this moment I had already gotten rid of my clothes. The only thing standing between me and her is what I'm wearing.

I extract myself from her quickly and remove my clothes faster than a teenage boy in the back of his parent's borrowed car. My cock is hard and pulsing as I drop my briefs to the ground. It springs free, begging for release. I look up and see Holly's eyes wide with excitement. She takes in my large cock, my hard muscles, and my tattoos. She devours me with those sexy eyes and it takes every ounce of strength I have not to blow my wad.

I reach for my jeans and pull a Magnum condom out of my wallet. I make quick work at sheathing myself before I'm hovering back against Holly's warm body. Her legs wrap around my waist again as if completely on their own. They feel so right there, like our bodies were made for each other.

I gaze deep into her eyes as I position myself at her entrance. Her mouth is open as she tries to suck in deep breaths of air. I slowly start to enter her. *Sweet Jeezus in Heaven!* Her body is tight as I feel her stretching to accommodate my girth. She feels so fucking amazing.

Her eyes are glued to mine as I slowly push in further. "Are you okay?" I whisper.

"Way more than okay," she replies with the slight curve up of her mouth. That mouth.

I'm on her mouth a second later. She tastes like heaven when she gasps against my mouth as I fill her completely. I'm all the way in, balls deep, and it couldn't be more perfect. My entire body is alive with crazy energy that I've never experienced before as I revel in the intimate connection we share.

Holly wiggles underneath me and my need to move takes over. I slowly pull out and push back in. She looks like a fucking goddess spread out underneath me. I run my hand from her side, up her chest, and to her neck. Holly moans as I stroke the soft skin of her neck. Her eyes keep fluttering closed as I slowly pick up the pace.

My need to take control is so great that I almost throw her hands above her head and ravish her body. *Slow, Jase.*

I decide to turn over. Grabbing Holly around the lower back, I flip us both over without breaking the sweet connection. Holly straddles me and sits up. Her body is smokin' but the image of her sitting on top of me, riding me the way she is, is fucking killing me. Her perky tits make my mouth water as I watch, helplessly, while she takes me for a ride. Our eyes remain locked. The emotions I see cross her face are both exciting and terrifying.

Just when I think she's about done being on top, I reach to grab for her, ready to flip her around again. But when she quickly spins around, that's when I almost blow it. She straddles me, facing my feet, and slowly slides down on me – Reverse Cowgirl. I literally have to start thinking about the last Executives meeting we had with management just to keep from coming. The feel of her body grinding down on me as she faces my feet is exquisite. I don't even realize at first that the moans filling the room are mine.

Just when I think I can't hang on any longer, I sit up and help spin Holly around so she's facing me again. She wraps her legs around me as I position my hands on her ass. I help her slide back down again. Her position as she sits on top of me makes her mouth is perfectly aligned for kissing. The kisses are urgent and hard as I continually move her up and down on my length. Holly wraps her arms firmly around my neck, riding me.

Just as I feel that familiar tightening at the base of my spine, I feel Holly begin to tighten around me. She drops down on me, grinding against me in the most delicious way. Her moans fill my ears and her body starts to shake against mine. I watch helpless as Holly sits back, staring deep into my eyes, and screws me into oblivion.

Her body is so tight around mine that I can't hold back my release. I give in, spilling myself into the confines of the condom and blowing my mind clear to kingdom come, as her pace slows until it eventually stops.

I wrap my arms firmly around her, pulling her flush against me. Our bodies mold together in a slick, sweaty way. Our breathing is both labored but it doesn't stop me from seeking out her lips with my own.

The kiss is sweet and soft. We're both spent, yet we both kiss like our lives depend on the touch of the other. I fucking love kissing her.

After several minutes, I lay back and pull her against me. Holly fits perfectly against me as I slide myself from her body causing us both to shiver at the instant loss. I absently stroke the hair at her forehead as we both start to drift. As much as I don't want to move, I need to get rid of the used condom and get us both underneath the covers. So, I hop up and exit her room, walking across the hall into the bathroom.

I'm back a few moments later and stare at the beauty before me. Holly's practically sleeping on the bed, beautifully naked and sated from our mind-blowing sex. My legs carry me quickly back to her bed. I tug the blankets back and move her so that she's underneath them with me next to her a second later. I pull her body snug against mine, her back to my front, as we start to drift off.

I want to say something, but I don't know what. The one thing I want to say would probably scare the shit out of her. Hell, it scares the shit out of me. I have feelings for this woman I've never experienced before – never dreamed could possibly exist so deep. I thought that maybe I'd been close to love once, but now that I know what love really feels like, before was nothing but a cheap knock-off imitation.

This? This is love.

It's official.

At twenty-six years old, I have officially had the best damn sex of my life and fallen in love. Nothing will ever top this.

But, I'll be damned if we don't try to top it

again in the early morning.

Chapter Thirteen

Holly

Saying goodbye to Jase was the hardest thing I've ever done. We woke just after four a.m. and took a shower. Together.

Something was slightly different with Jase once we woke up this morning. He held me close like I was a treasure. He kissed me deeply and thoroughly as he savored the touch of our lips. Several times he acted like he had more to say, but he never said it.

I'm walking down the corridor towards the emergency room in a lovesick trance. If there was one thing I realized when Jase left this morning it was that I didn't just care for him, I was falling in love with him. Heck, I was probably already there. The thought of not seeing him in person again until June, is wreaking havoc on my heart.

"Holly," I hear from behind.

I know the voice, so when I turn to see Avery's brother, Will, standing in front of me, I can't help the smile that spreads across my face.

"Hey, Will. How's it going?"

"Listen, we need to talk," Will says urgently as he gently tugs my arm towards an open exam room in the back of the emergency department.

"What's up?" I ask cautiously, worried that something is wrong with Avery or one of the kids.

"Have you seen the news?" he asks, concern etched across his handsome face. A face that at one time, I thought might be the face I'd wake up to every morning. Will and I have never had a relationship, but for awhile, I thought of him as more than a friend. I think Avery was a big part of that. It seemed like she kept trying to push us together. It didn't take long before the feelings I had for him slowly faded, and I realized that Will and I would be nothing more than friends.

"No. I've been here for the past four hours. Why?" I ask, looking over his shoulder as I hear a commotion in the hallway.

"It's all over the news, Holly. Your relationship with Jase," he says with sad eyes.

"What? How is that possible?" I ask.

"They caught video of him at the airport just a bit ago. Apparently, someone took pictures of you and Jase on the street in front of the café in town," he says with a knowing look.

Shit. Jase and I were sucking face hardcore on the sidewalk in front of the café! "Oh crap, Will. Really?"

"Yeah, really. They have several pictures including some of you guys at dinner last night and him walking you up to your door and going inside. Then, they have him exiting your condo this morning, giving you a goodbye kiss, and driving away."

"Please tell me you're kidding," I whisper as my throat becomes so dry, I can barely speak. My heart is lodged firmly in my throat.

"I wish I was, kid. National media is descending upon Rivers Edge as we speak. They found out just a bit ago that you work here. The media is camped outside the hospital trying to get pictures or interviews with you," he says.

"This is not happening," I mumble, dropping my head in my hands.

"Afraid it is," he says as he pulls me into a hug.

A flash, followed by a commotion outside the hallway draws our attention again, and I see one of the security guards pulling a grinning photographer away from the doorway. In the hallway, several other security guards are pushing back about four men and women with cameras and microphones.

As soon as I step into the hallway, questions are hurdled at me in a rapid-fire manner.

"Are you Jase Bentley's girlfriend?"

"How long have you been the other woman?"

"How did you meet Jase Bentley?"

Will pulls me back inside the small exam room. My entire body starts to shake as the realization that my normal little life has been turned upside down. "I'm calling Carmen. You have to get out of here," he says as he makes his way over to the phone on the wall.

After a few minutes of talking to our boss on the other end, Will approaches me. "I'm taking you home. We'll take my car since I'm sure they already know what you drive," he says as he guides me towards the back entrance of the emergency room.

Will opens the door and looks around, not seeing anyone in the back lot. He takes my hand and pulls me towards the parking area. As soon as we reach the edge of the lot, a group of voices ring out behind me. I glance over my shoulder just as several photographers come around the side of the hospital. Will sees them, too, and we begin to run. He already has his keys out and ready when we reach his car. He's shoving me inside the passenger seat moments before he runs around to the driver's side. With the ignition started, Will pulls out of the spot as the car is inundated by the press.

We're both quiet as Will drives quickly towards my condo. Will is very familiar with the neighborhood because he actually lives only two condos down from mine. In fact, it was Will who passed along word that the condo I now call home was available.

Will pulls into the empty driveway. "Get your keys ready," he instructs as he looks around. "Let's go now before they get here," he adds as he exits his side of the car. I'm out and running towards my front door just as the first vehicle pulls up.

Will takes the keys from my shaking hand and inserts it into my lock and turns. As soon as it releases, he's thrusting me forward and into my living room. With a quick flip of the lock, we're secured within my condo. Will walks around and closes the blinds and curtains so that we are hidden from prying eyes. I'm shaking like a leaf, arms wrapped firmly around my torso, as if I can somehow warm myself up.

"You're shaking," Will says as he pulls me back into his embrace. He's as tall as Jase. Will is almost as tall as his two older brothers and the same height as his younger one.

"I can't seem to get warm," I whisper against his hard chest.

Will looks down at me through his wire-rimmed glasses. Blue eyes that are the same as his siblings bore into me. "Come on, Holl. Let's get you on the couch, and I'll call someone," he says as he steers me towards my couch.

I wrap myself in the throw blanket as Will grabs his cell phone from the front pocket of his navy blue uniform pants. His fingers fly across his screen before he puts it up to his ears.

"Hey, it's me. Yeah, we have a situation," Will says into the phone. I know exactly who he's calling.

"She's fine and home. Her yard is crawling with media though," he says.

"Okay, see ya in a few," he says just before hanging up.

"Ave is on her way," he tells me as he sits down next to me on the couch. "She's running the
148

kids to Mom's house first since Maddox is working. She's calling him now and having him come over to clear a path."

"Can't he just flex his muscles and make them leave?" I ask.

"I don't think that's how it works, Holl. I think as long as they stay on public property, like the sidewalks and the street, they can't do anything about it."

I make a face at him, disgusted at the thought of the media invading my life like this. "We'll talk to Maddox and Jake as soon as they get here," he adds as he pats my knee.

Ten minutes later, Maddox and Jake pull up in their police cruiser. Jake works the crowd, reminding them to stay off of private property while Maddox makes his way to my place. Will opens the door immediately for him while I keep my post on the couch.

"Hey, Holl. You alright?" Maddox says as he enters the living room and takes a look around.

I watch my best friend's husband for several moments before I answer. "Yeah, I'm good." *I wish Jase was here*, I think to myself.

Speaking of Jase, I should probably call him. He should be back on the east coast by now and is probably well aware of the situation. Before I can get up and search for my cell phone, my front door bursts open as Avery flies in.

I jump off the couch and she has me enveloped in a fierce hug a split second later. There's nothing like the comforts of a best friend. Avery has been the one to laugh with me - sometimes at me - cry with me, and hold my hand. And likewise, I've done the same for her many times over. Nothing beats the love I have for her and her family. Well, except maybe the love I'm developing for a certain dark haired, green eyed rocker.

"Are you okay?" she asks as she pulls back a little and looks down at my tear streaked face. I didn't even realize I was crying.

"Yeah, I'm okay. This whole thing is just crazy, you know? Why are they here? Why do they care about me?" I ask the group as a whole.

"I don't think it's particularly you, Holly. They're interested in the dirt on Jase and *you* just happen to be that dirt," Avery says as she leads us both to the couch.

"They're taking my picture everywhere I go. I don't think I can live like that, Ave," I mumble. "I want to be able to go to work and do my job without someone putting a camera in my face. I want to be able to get gas without someone asking me a bunch of questions that they have no business knowing the answers to."

"I know, sweetie. Have you talked to Jase?" Avery asks.

"No, I was just getting up to look for my phone when you came in," I say, looking for my purse.

"I've got it right here, Holly," Will says as he walks over from where he and Maddox were talking by the kitchen.

"Jake?" I ask, looking around and still not seeing the eldest Stevens brother.

"Outside making sure all of the photographers stay off your lawn," Maddox says as he finally approaches his wife. He kneels down and pulls her into his arms as Will hands me my phone. I try not to watch their moment together, but I always find myself being sucked in like a moth to a flame. Avery and Maddox are so dang passionate and loving that you can't help but watch, envious.

"Thanks, Will," I say as I power my phone back up. I had shut it off in the hospital when our new boss, Carmen, was lurking around, watching all of us like hawks. No wonder everyone calls her

Cruella behind her back.

When the phone is finally powered up, I see fourteen missed calls and about twenty text messages. With the exception of two missed calls from Avery and another from my sister, all of the contacts are from Jase.

I excuse myself and head into my room so I can talk to him in private. I push the familiar keys and send the call. Jase answers on the first ring.

"Holly?" he asks, his tone a combination of fear and relief.

"Hey," I reply into the phone. My entire body calms at the sound of his voice. I drop down on my bed as the tears well in my eyes.

"Baby, are you alright?"

"Yeah, I'm fine. I got sent home from work today because the media was everywhere. They snuck into the hospital and were snapping pictures at me. My lawn is covered with people with cameras. What is going on, Jase?"

"Apparently, I was followed or someone there tipped them off. Our pictures are all over the television. I don't want to scare you, baby, but more people are probably descending on Rivers Edge as we speak," he adds.

"Where are you?"

"New York. As soon as I got off the plane, the paparazzi were waiting for me. They didn't have your name yet, though I think they do now. They're throwing it around like money."

I groan as I lay back on the bed.

"Babe, hold on. Phil just walked in and wants me to watch something on the television," Jase says. I hear the man in the background and hear the sounds of the TV.

I don't have a TV in my room because I knew if I did, I would just stay up late watching some mindless reality program. Sleep is too valuable to me.

"Holly, who is the guy?" Jase asks a moment later, his voice tense and curt.

"What? Who?" I reply.

"The guy you're hugging and holding hands with," he says again in the same tone. He sounds cold.

It only takes a few minutes before it dawns on me who he's talking about. "Oh, that's Will," I reply matter-of-factly.

"Who the hell is Will?" he asks, his voice rising slightly, filled with edge.

"That's one of Avery's brothers. He works with me. I've known him for years," I tell him, confused by his reaction to Will.

"Are you seeing him?" he seethes through gritted teeth.

"Will? No!" I defend, sitting up from my bed.

"Have you ever dated him?"

"Why are you doing this, Jase?"

"Answer the question, Holly. Have you ever dated Will?"

"I guess, technically, once. He took me to my senior prom when my date backed out last minute," I whisper.

He's quiet for a few seconds before finally asking, "Is he the one you used to love?"

My mind is racing. "Jase, what are you doing?" I ask, not understanding any of this at all. Where the hell is my Jase?

"I've been messed around on by women for years, Holly. I'm not about to let you fuck with me, too," Jase growls into the phone.

"What are you talking about?" I say with raised voice.

"You and Will are all over the news, Holly. They have pictures of you two going back for years. They have pictures of you two from today. They're calling you two lovers," he says, whispering the last sentence as he sounds dejected and spent.

"Will and I have always been friends, Jase. Nothing more. Did I want more at one time? Yes. Did Will ever want more? No. Was I in love with him years ago? Yes. But that was years ago, Jase. Like high school, puppy love kind of love."

"He was your first love, wasn't he," he asks, sadness filling his quiet voice.

"Yeah, but it was unrequited and it was years ago, Jase. You are acting nuts," I tell him, pacing around my bedroom.

"Well, it just looks a little weird, Holly," Jase says in a defensive tone.

"Things aren't as they seem through the eyes of the media. You're the one who taught me that," I exhale loudly and close my eyes. Jase is still quiet on the other end of the line and I don't give him the chance to talk. "Listen, this isn't working out for me. This isn't what I signed up for. I don't want my personal life spilled all over the world. I don't want people chasing me around with cameras. I don't want my trips to the grocery store to be featured in Entertainment News. And most of all, I don't want to be with someone who doesn't know me well enough to know that I would never, ever cheat. So, I think this is where we part ways, Jase."

The other end is silence as tears silently fall unchecked down my cheek.

"Holly, I do trust you," Jase says. He sounds so small.

"Jase, I can't do this anymore. It's been mere hours of being in the public life and I don't want it. I want out," I whisper.

"If you want out then there's nothing more I can say," he whispers back.

"Goodbye, Jase."

"Yeah, bye," he says before signing off the call.

I silently cry for fifteen minutes before I pull myself together to face my friends. I walk out into the living room where Avery and Will are watching the entertainment channel. My face is plastered everywhere. Hugging Will. Running with Will to his car. Making out with Jase on my front porch.

The host is talking about an interview with Camille Douglas moments before the screen cuts to the interview. Camille is standing outside of her condo, smiling perfectly for the camera.

"I suspected that Jase was cheating on me throughout the relationship which is why I ended it with him. So to know that his mistress had her own affair is rather poetic, don't you think?" Camille says as she smiles that million dollar smile.

Great. So, first I'm a home wrecker and now a slut. Awesome.

I close my eyes as Avery turns off the television and turns to face me. "Were you talking to Jase?" Avery asks, her eyes filled with concern.

"Yeah," I reply on autopilot.

"What did he say about all of this?" Avery asks.

"We didn't really get to talk too much about that part. We kinda broke up," I say, allowing the words to wash over me. The tears leak from my eyes before I can even fight them off.

"What?" she exclaims as she charges at me. "Because of the Will thing?" she asks, turning back towards her brother. I give my friend a questioning look before she adds, "We heard you mention his name a few times while you were on the phone."

"I'll call him and talk to him, Holly," Will offers as he approaches.

"No, it's okay. If he can't believe me when I say that you and I are only friends, that's his problem. Not mine. Besides, that was only part of it. I just don't think I can handle this lifestyle, you know?" I don't look up and make eye contact with Avery. I know she'll see right through me.

"Hey, Will, can you give us a minute?" Avery asks over her shoulder.

"Sure. I'll be in the kitchen," he says as he walks away.

Avery pulls me towards the couch and all but pushes me down onto the cushions. "Talk," she demands.

"Jase kept asking about Will and about all the pictures. The other side of the story is that there are just as many pictures on Facebook of me with your other brothers, too, over the years. The problem was that he believed that I was capable of being with someone else while I was with him," I choke on the words as they leave my mouth.

It's silent for several minutes until Avery finally says, "Have you told him that you love him?"

I look up, my heart breaking into shards of nothing all over again as I shake my head no.

"Why did you say you weren't ready for this lifestyle? It's not like you weren't expecting it. You knew when you entered this relationship that it was going to turn into this, right?"

"Yeah, I knew. I wasn't prepared for it when it finally happened, but I knew."

"So why did you tell him it was why you were breaking up?"

"Because it seemed like the only way to cut ties with him and he'd actually let me go."

"I'm confused. Why do you want him to let you go, Holl?" she asks, putting her hand on my knee, as her eyes search mine looking for a hint of understanding.

"Because eventually he'll realize that I'm nothing special. Eventually he would realize that and leave anyway. At least I did it my own way before my heart got completely shattered," I say.

"But see, I don't think your heart walked away unscathed. I think you're already so far in love with him you can't see straight. Am I right?"

Acknowledging the truth sucks. Avery sucks.

I shake my head up and down. God, I hate it when she's right. It's so much better when we're dissecting her life and not mine.

"So, now what?" she asks.

"I don't know. The fact that he still doesn't trust me and that he believes the story those pictures are telling is a deal breaker for me. I just gave him the out," I say.

"Give it a day or so and then talk to him," she advises.

"We'll see," I mumble. "Look, you guys have families to get to. I'll be fine here, and I really just want to be alone anyway," I tell Avery.

"Are you sure? I can stay or Will?"

"No, I'm good. Thanks," I say as I stand up and hug my best friend.

Will and Maddox enter the room and give me a quick hug before they all head towards the door. "Call me if you need anything?" she says.

"Absolutely," I reply with a forced grin.

I watch as my best friend and her brother leave and head towards their respective vehicles. While the street is filled with cars and people, my driveway is completely empty since my car is still at the hospital. Oh well, I'll worry about getting it later. It's not like I can go anywhere, anyway.

I settle in for a long, quiet day. I can't read because I can't concentrate long enough to absorb the words. I can't watch television because my face is plastered all over every channel. I can't go for a walk because dozens of photographers are ready to pounce on me outside.

I grab my pillow and lie down on the couch. My pillow that smells like Jase. The tears fall into the soft material as I lay on the couch, absorbed in my own misery and grief.

This is what I wanted. Alone.

No, what I want is Jase. Happiness.

I just made sure I can never have it again.

Chapter Fourteen

Jase

The tour drags on. It's torture to get up every day. Torture to walk up on stage. Torture to smile for the camera like my world isn't completely crushed into a million fucking pieces. Ever since Holly said she couldn't handle my life, I've been broken. So broken that I fear I'll never be whole again. Not without Holly.

I'm down to my final concert of the tour tomorrow night and it's a big one. Madison Square Garden. Bent is going out with a bang. The biggest show of our career. The one stadium we have yet to play.

I just wish Holly was going to be there to see it.

I'm buttoning up the buttons on the front of my blue plaid shirt while I wait for my designated time slot for makeup. I'm guest starring on the Amanda Knows Show tonight. Amanda is the newest nighttime talk show host with skyrocketing ratings each and every night. Tonight, Amanda and I are supposed to discuss the final stop of the tour and I'm going to sing the newest release with Bent, but I know that Amanda is going to drill me about this past month. Hell, everyone has been chomping at the bit to question me over it.

I've kept a very low profile since I left Rivers Edge. The last thing I wanted was to bring more media attention and scrutiny to Holly back home. The media has been cruel to her and painted the ugliest picture possible. I can't stomach the things they're saying about her. About us. The time I shared with her was the best part of my life and I can't fucking stand to listen to them taint it.

This past month has been hell. Mostly because I realized that I was completely wrong about her and that guy. I knew before I opened my big fat mouth that Holly wasn't seeing him, yet I couldn't stop myself from letting my emotions - my fears - take over. I saw those pictures of her and Will on her Facebook page, along with the dozens of other pictures with the Stevens family. I knew they were just friends, and I did the one thing that I don't allow myself to do. I let the media inside my relationship.

I fucked everything up. Bad.

I've picked up my phone at least a dozen times every single day to call her. Instead, I just look at her face on my screen from the night we met. That beautiful face that I still dream about every night. It haunts me like the Ghost of What Could Have Been. That ghost is a bitch.

When she told me she that she couldn't handle my lifestyle, I decided right then and there to let her go. I can't force her to handle it, you know? Then why in the hell am I so fucking miserable and why does my heart keep screaming at me to open my eyes?

A knock sounds on the door followed by a quick, "Five minutes."

I grab my phone and look down at her picture one more time like I do every free moment of every single day. I start to put it back in my pocket, when I decide to scroll through my contacts. It's as if my fingers are acting on their own. Helping to fix the fuck ups I've created.

Avery.

Without allowing myself one second to think it through, I quickly hit 'Call'.

Avery's voice fills my ear after the third ring. "Hello?"

"Hey, Avery. It's Jase," I tell her.

She's quiet for several seconds and I start to wonder if we lost connection. "Jase?"

"Yeah," I say as I clear my throat.

"What's up?" she asks, her voice friendly and not full of the hostility that I expected.

"I, uh…I'm not sure why I called," I tell her honestly.

"She's doing okay," she says as she closes a door, closing herself off from the kids in the background.

"Really?" I ask, glad at least that she's okay while I wallow in my misery.

"I mean, she's as good as can be expected considering she's miserable."

"She is?" I ask, perking up for the first time in weeks. Sadistic bastard that I am is actually a little relieved that she hasn't completely moved on with her life as if I wasn't a part of it.

"Yeah, she is. How about you?"

"Fucking wrecked," I tell her honestly. "I can't eat. I can't sleep. I can't breathe."

"Why haven't you called her?" she asks.

I don't know. Because I'm an idiot. "I don't know what to say."

"Well, start with the truth," she says.

"The truth still doesn't change the fact that

165

she can't deal with my life," I reply, dejected all over again.

"Think about that for a few minutes, Jase. Really think about it."

I sit there with my eyes closed. Holly's laugh. Holly's sparkling hazel eyes. Holly's smile as she sasses back to me. Holly underneath me as we made love. The look in her eyes while we connected so much deeper than we've both ever connected with anyone else before. As if there was never anyone else before. As if we were the only two people in the entire world.

And then I know. I know she loves me. She loves me for me, not Jase Bentley - lead singer of Bent. Holly is the only one who truly knows the real me. The stress. The restlessness. The loneliness. She knows all of that and loves me anyway. She's the only one I've ever let in.

"Does she still love me, Avery?" I ask, hopeful and terrified all at the same time.

"What do you think, Jase?" she replies, the smile in her voice as evident as the earth under my feet.

"I've gotta go," I tell her and start to pull my phone down. "Wait!" I say as I bring the phone back up to my ear. "Avery?"

"Yeah?"

"Can you make sure Holly is watching the Amanda Knows Show tonight?"

"I think I can do that," she replies with happiness in each word.

"Thanks, Avery. I owe you."

"You make my best friend as happy as she deserves to be and that's all the thanks I need," she says.

"Deal," I reply before I click off the phone.

"Makeup, Mr. Bentley," I hear as the knock sounds on the door.

I shove my phone into my pocket and head out of the small dressing room. I follow the young assistant as he walks me back to makeup.

Thirty minutes to show time.

Jesse is sitting in the seat next to me when I get in there. "Change in plan," I tell him. Jesse looks up and just raises his eyebrow at me. "The new song we've ran through a couple of times? I want to do that tonight."

"What? We can't change our song last minute, Jase. We've ran through that song, like what, three times?" Jesse says as the makeup artist applies powder to his face.

167

"We are. I'm singing that song tonight, Jesse."

"For the girl?" he asks with the slightest raise of the corner of his mouth.

"What girl?" I ask, knowing damn good and well who he's referring to.

"The girl you wrote that song for," he says with a smile.

I just smile back at him.

Yes, it's about that girl. My girl.

The only girl.

*****

"And now, please help me welcome Jase Bentley," Amanda says from her seat behind the small desk.

The crowd erupts into loud cheers as I walk out onto the stage. I give them all my patented smile and offer a little wave to the crowd before stepping up and towards the seat next to Amanda's desk. Amanda stands up and gives me a friendly hug over the desk before waving her hand and indicating for me to have a seat.

168

"Jase Bentley, everyone," she says with a huge smile.

"Thanks for having me, Amanda," I say with a grin.

"Jase, Jase, Jase. You've been a very busy man for awhile now. How's the tour?" she asks.

"Really great," I say. "Though, it's actually wrapping up tomorrow night here in New York City," I say with a smile.

"Sad? Happy?"

"Sad to see it coming to an end, but happy at the same time," I reply.

"What does that mean?"

"Well, I will miss the guys. I will miss the fans. I will miss making music. But, I'm ready to take a step back. I'm ready to find roots and settle down a little bit."

"So the rumors are true? Bent is taking a hiatus for awhile?"

"That is true," I start to say as the crowd shares their displeasure with rounds of boos. "I'm not sure for how long, but I definitely need a break. It's been crazy. I've been on the road for three years straight and while I'm grateful for the opportunities we've had, it's time to step back and live our lives outside of the spotlight every night."

"Does this have anything to do with a certain woman you were photographed with a month back?" she asks with a sly smile. I knew she was going to bring her up.

I smile back at Amanda. She's tall - about five foot, eight - with long brown hair and chocolate brown eyes. She's also about thirty-five years old and has worked as a correspondence for several entertainment news agencies before she was offered this primetime spot.

"I'd been thinking about it for about six months before I met the woman in those photos."

Amanda sets her chin on her fist and leans in ready to get the scoop. "So, let's talk about that woman, Jase. Who is she?"

"She is a woman I met two months ago before a show in St. Charles. She stole my breath the first moment I saw her," I tell her.

"So, you were seeing her?"

"Despite what you might have heard, I had no clue who she was before that night. I also was not seeing Camille by that point either."

"Ahhhhh, Camille. I remember those accusations she flung your way. So, you weren't dating her anymore, right?"

"No, I had broken it off with Camille a week before I met that woman in Missouri," I tell her.

"So, what's going on with the two of you now?"

"Unfortunately, nothing," I tell her. "My life is very public and it's a hard life for those who aren't used to it to deal with. I don't blame her at all for walking away," I tell Amanda.

"Wait! She walked away?" she asks, incredulous as the crowd echoed her astonishment.

"Yeah, she did," I reply and look down.

"You seem regretful of that, Jase."

"I am very much regretful of that. I have so much I want to say to her."

"Why don't you tell her now?" she asks with a huge wolfish grin. Ratings!

"As much as I'd love to, Amanda, I actually would prefer to tell her in person, face to face, without the audience," I say with a laugh.

"Awww, that's too bad. So, what can we expect for Bent's final show tomorrow night?" Amanda asks.

"We are tearing up Madison Square Garden tomorrow night. I'm told the show has been sold out for months, but I have a pair of tickets to one lucky audience member this evening," I say causing the entire crowd to erupt to eardrum splitting decibels.

"That's so great, Jase. We'll help you pick a winner of those tickets in just a bit. Did I hear that you and Bent are going to sing a song for us tonight?" she asks.

"You heard correct," I reply as I start to stand up.

Bent is already in position on stage right so I start to head over to my friends, my band. I slide my familiar guitar around my neck and step up to the microphone.

"Ladies and gentleman, I present to you, Bent," Amanda says, offering us a round of applause.

"Thank you, Amanda. You know, we were going to perform our latest release, 'Trigger Finger', but I have a real treat for you tonight. Tonight, we're performing a new song that I wrote a few weeks back. It's called 'Promise Me'," I say.

The drums count down the beat as the guitars slowly play the melody I wrote. It's soft and instrumental and speaks from the soul.

Beautiful eyes, eyes that fill my nights with brightness,

Stunning smile, a smile that livens up my days,

The softest skin, as you wrap your arms around me,

Filling my heart with only you in so many ways.

I feel your body press against me,

Lighting me up like never before,

I crave your touch, your light, your laughter,

I crave your love forever more.

Promise me, you'll always be beside me

Promise me, that you will always see us through,

I promise you to love you always,

I promise you, only you.

Promise me,

I promise you.

The lyrics flow as I close my eyes and picture her face. I sing this song only for her and I pray that somewhere, somehow she is watching. I pray that she is listening to these words and knows they are for her. I pray that she knows all of the things I never told her.

This is her song. My ballad. The only love ballad I've ever written, and it is hers. The only one I will ever write because there will never be another after her.

She's it.

My life.

My forever song.

*****

"Last show," Phillip says behind me.

"Yep," I reply as I strap my guitar around my neck.

"You gonna miss this?" he asks, nodding towards the darkened arena. The crowd is electric as they chant the name Bent, Bent, Bent over and over again.

I smile as I answer, "I'll miss it, sure. But, I'm ready to wake up tomorrow and not have an agenda of things to do."

"Yeah, well, find yourself a wife and kids

and I guarantee you'll never have a moment to yourself again," he says with a laugh.

I laugh in return. "You're probably right. And if I get a chance at that wife and kids, I'm latching on as tight as humanly possible. I'm not letting her go again," I say moments before stepping out on the stage.

The lights are dark, but I follow the stage lights to my spot in front. The band is counting down the start of "Fire." I start the lyrics for the final time. The thought tightens my chest and catches my breath. The last time.

And I'm okay with that.

I glance around the crowd, only able to see the first few rows because of the blinding lights. I'm actually losing my mind because the girl in the front row actually looks like Holly. Over the last month, I've seen her everywhere, in every city. I close my eyes and finish the song without looking back. Seeing a woman who resembles her is the worst kind of torture. Punishment.

I make it through four more songs before I have to walk away. Those hazel eyes are so intense and fierce, so much like Holly's. She's been staring at me the entire concert, not singing along, not moving. Just staring. I'm starting to think I'm losing my fucking mind.

I signal to the band that I'm going to play "Promise Me". We played it for the first time publicly last night on the Amanda Knows Show and it seems fitting that we play it one last time tonight.

I grab the stool at the back of the stage and pull it up front and center.

"Hey, you guys don't mind if I sit for a minute, do you?" I ask the audience. Their deafening screams fill my ears and I can't help the smile that spreads wide across my face. I'm going to miss this part of touring. I'm going to miss interacting with the fans who just came to hear me sing. The music. It reaches deep into your soul and touches you in ways that nothing else can.

"Recently, I wrote a song that I thought I'd sing for you guys tonight. Since this is Bent's final show for awhile, I thought it'd be only fitting that you guys get to hear it live and in person tonight. Is that okay?" I ask the screaming crowd.

Jesse starts the now familiar cords of the intro.

I close my eyes and let the words flow.

Beautiful eyes, eyes that fill my nights with brightness,

Stunning smile, a smile that livens up my

days,

The softest skin, as you wrap your arms around me,

Filling my heart, with only you in so many ways.

I feel your body press against me,

Lighting me up like never before,

I crave your touch, your light, your laughter,

I crave your love forever more.

I open my eyes as I sing that last line and my eyes instantly connect with that girl who reminds me so much of my Holly. The girl has tears streaming down her face. That perfect heart-shaped face that I picture everywhere I go. Those deep, hazel eyes that are like windows to her soul. That lush, warm mouth that I dream about kissing at all hours of the day.

Suddenly, I stop singing. I watch helplessly as that girl - the Holly look-alike - starts to move from her seat, excusing herself as she moves around the standing people as she heads towards the aisle. She never takes her eyes off of me as she makes her way to the corner of the stage, politely pushing her way through the throngs of people. Security stops her at the edge of the stage, holding her back just before she actually reaches my location.

And that's when I know. I know it so clearly and deeply. Like the clouds opening up and letting the sunshine through for the first time in days. Weeks. It's Holly. My Holly.

She's here.

I jump up off the stool and run towards the corner of the stage where security is trying to escort her back to her seat.

"Wait, wait, wait," I yell as I approach their location.

The security guard and Holly both look up at the same time and see me squatting on the stage. "She's with me," I say as I extend my hand down to her, holding my breath as I wait.

Her smile could light up the entire arena, and I'm pretty sure mine is the exact mirror image. Holly extends her hand upward. Electricity flares through my body as we touch for the first time in a month. I feel alive. I can breathe – really breathe - for the first time in weeks.

The security guard helps lift Holly onto the stage. The crowd is on their feet screaming and cheering, but I don't hear them. I only hear Holly's short pants of breath. I lead her over towards my stool, center stage. Flashes from cell phones and cameras are everywhere and bright enough to blind you, but neither of us take our eyes off of each other for one second.

A second stool appears out of nowhere. Okay, not out of nowhere - Jesse delivers the stool with a big smug smile on his face. Jackass.

I guide Holly to sit in the seat I just vacated and turn her so that she's facing me. I move my stool and my body so that I'm facing directly at her. I set my guitar on my lap, keeping my eyes locked on her tear-filled ones, and finish the song.

Promise me, you'll always be beside me

Promise me, that you will always see us through,

I promise you to love you always,

I promise you, only you.

Promise me,

I promise you.

The band never joins in. I sing the rest of my song acoustic style to the girl I wrote it for. Just me, Holly, and my guitar. And twenty-thousand screaming fans.

As soon as I strum the final note, I remove

my guitar and set it on the ground. My pulse is skyrocketing to stroke level. Holly's crying eyes are filled with so much love and adoration that I know deep down that there is no way I will ever be able to walk away from this woman. No way will I ever let my stupid pride get in the way of the best thing to ever walk into my Meet and Greet, into my life.

No way will I ever let her go.

Chapter Fifteen

Holly

You'd think I'd be embarrassed to be sitting up on stage with thousands of screaming Bent fans staring at me. But as long as I keep my eyes locked on Jase's striking green eyes, I don't even know the rest exists.

Jase sets his guitar down on the stage and leans towards me. His hands feel amazing. Like the missing piece of my life has finally clicked into place. I can't help the big smile that spreads across my face. A smile that I haven't seen in almost a month - well, until last night when Avery insisted I watched his interview and performance on Amanda Knows Show.

Jase gets up from his stool and stands directly in front of me. Our fingers link together as we continue to have a conversation with our eyes. Neither of us say a word, yet we know exactly what the other is thinking. We just connect like that.

"I fucked up pretty bad," he finally says with a slight lift of the corner of his lip. "I knew that there was nothing going on with you and your friend, but I couldn't stop myself from making an ass out of myself. I couldn't stop myself from hurting you and insulting you the way I did. There's no excuse for it, Holly, and I'm so damn sorry.

"From the first moment I picked up a guitar at age six, I knew I had found love. Music. That was my first and only love. Until you. Until you walked into that Meet and Greet, and I saw you standing across the room. I knew that my first love was now my second. I knew that I had found the one thing I had been searching for and didn't even know it. I found you.

"Tonight, I'm going to walk off this stage for the final time. It's going to be the hardest thing I've done, and while I'm happy to have the break, it still terrifies me. The only thing that could make this night any better is to walk off this stage towards you. You are my music. You are my first," he says to me and only me. You wouldn't even know that there are thousands of fans watching right now because besides the occasional clicking of a camera, you could hear a pin drop in Madison Square Garden.

"I don't have a ring," he tells me as he slowly drops down on one knee. "I'm not proposing to you tonight - though that's coming soon. Tonight, I'm making you a promise. Tonight, I promise to love you until I take my last breath. Tonight, I promise to hold your hand when you laugh and wipe your tears when you cry. Tonight, I promise that every ounce of my being belongs to you and always will."

I watch as he sucks in a deep breath. My eyes are riveted to him, pulled in to the endless depths of those green eyes. Eyes that speak to me just as much as the words coming from his mouth.

"A month ago you promised me that you would stick by me and I'm holding you to that promise. I can't let you go, Holly. You are my air, my light, my water, and my fucking world," Jase confesses as I stare down at the only man I've ever really, truly, honestly loved.

"And I love you so much it fucking hurts," he adds.

Tears from my eyes drop down onto our linked fingers. "You have nothing to apologize for, Jase. We both messed up. I lied to you when I told you that I couldn't deal with all of this. I lied because I was scared. The truth is I can deal with it. I want to deal with it. Because having to deal with the madness you call your life is so much better than not having you in mine at all. I choose you," I whisper. "And I love you, too."

Jase is standing before I even realize what is going on. I'm engulfed in a big hug, wrapped tightly in his hard, sweaty arms. His lips taste and feel like heaven. His breath washes over me as he kisses me like I've never been kissed before. And considering the first few kisses we've shared, that's saying something.

After several minutes into our little make out session, Jase and I both finally come up for air, realizing exactly where we are. The crowd is electric as it starts to come back into focus. The other members of Bent are all smiling and clapping along with the audience. The intensity in Jase's green eyes is all-consuming.

"Promise me you'll always be right here with me. No matter how stupid I get or what asinine things I do, promise me," he says against my lips. "This is it - you and me for the rest of our lives."

"I promise," I whisper before his lips are back on mine in the best kiss. A kiss that signifies the rest of our lives.

*****

July 4ᵗʰ

"Babe, get out here with the rest of us and enjoy the party," Jase says from the back door of our new home. Jase purchased seventy-five acres of timber and open pasture outside of Rivers Edge as soon as the tour wrapped up. The older colonial, two story home is set far enough back from the road that you can't see it unless you come up the driveway. The first thing Jase did was hire Travis and his guys to install a security gate, subtle yet protective fencing, and sensors around the property. Then, while Jase took care of selling his place in California and making all the arrangements to move his permanent residence to Rivers Edge, Stevens Construction gave the older home a beautiful facelift. It's sparkling white with country blue shutters. The brand new wrap around porch is perfect for enjoying quiet, summer nights. Everything happened very fast and it still shocks me that Travis and his guys were able to complete everything so quickly. But, I guess when you have someone like Jase Bentley who will pay any amount of money for fast turnaround, you don't turn down the business.

We've officially lived here - together - for

three days. We moved in just in time to host our first official event - a July 4th party that was in the works while the updates were happening. My family is here, and Jase's family flew in for the holiday weekend. I had talked with most of them over the phone, but it was nice to finally get everyone together and all meet face to face. Plus, my extended family - the Stevens' - are all here to celebrate our nation's birthday.

"I'm coming," I say as I finish refilling the chips and dip tray. I walk over to the backdoor, lay a quick kiss on his oh-so-delicious lips, and follow him into our newly furnished backyard.

Jase and I went to St. Charles on my day off earlier in the week and purchased tables and chairs, lounges, a stationary double swing, and a massive swing set for the kids that took the guys two days and a lot of beer to construct. Brooklyn hasn't been off the swing set since she got here two hours ago. It warms my heart to see my honorary niece enjoying my place so much. After all, I would do anything for her - and her brother.

"Here's more chips and dip," I tell our family and friends as I set it down in the middle of the food table. Travis and Jake both jump up with their plates and practically push each other over to get to the homemade guacamole dip. I'll admit,

Mrs. Stevens is killer in the kitchen.

"Holly, how were your first few nights in the new house?" Erin asks from her bench seat next to Jake.

"Really great," I reply as I sit down at the large round table across from her. "Our first dinner was homemade mashed potatoes and mac and cheese," I add.

"That's an interesting combination. Are you pregnant?" Josselyn asks jokingly – or maybe not so jokingly – as she snuggles her eight month old.

"No. It's my favorite food and Jase's. It just felt right to do our two favorite foods on our first night in our new house together," I say, leaving out the part about nibbling that food off of each other's bodies.

"I think it's incredibly romantic. Who knew tattooed rocker, Jase Bentley, was such a sweetheart," Avery says from next to me.

"He is a big softy," I add with a smile, looking over at Jase who is in deep conversation with Will.

"And it helps that he's hot as hell," Erin says under her breath, yet not quite soft enough for her over-protective fiancé to not hear.

Lacey Black

"Seriously?" he asks.

"Oh, yeah," Josselyn replies as Erin giggles.

"Don't worry, cowboy. You're still my number one hottie," Erin says with a little grin as Jake leans over and kisses the crown of her head.

Two hours later, after all of the hamburgers and brats have been consumed and the kids are starting to settle down for the evening, Mrs. Stevens addresses the crowd. "Everyone, dusk is upon us. Why don't we all grab our blankets and chairs and settle in the yard to watch the fireworks."

Our yard should have a perfect view of the Rivers Edge fireworks off in the distance over the tree line. I jump up and grab one of the blankets piled on the patio for the evening. Jase is talking to Maddox and Nate so I head over and lay our blanket out on the ground. Everyone else appears to choose places towards the front, so I hang back a little bit. Part of enjoying our first holiday together is watching our families and friends enjoy the moment with us.

As soon as the blanket is stretched out, Jase joins me, flopping down on his back. His legs are extended out, tattooed arms back behind his head. He looks all sorts of comfortable, and I all of

188

a sudden wish we were alone.

"Quit looking at me like that or I'll have to throw you over my shoulder, march you to the house in front of our family and friends, and make you see your own fireworks," Jase says with that cocky smile I love so much.

"Fireworks, huh? Pretty sure of yourself there, big boy," I tease.

"You know it," he replies as I sit down next to him on the blanket. I watch my parents sit in lawn chairs with Jase's parents. My best friend holds her sleeping son on their blanket while Maddox continually lights sparklers for Brooklyn. The rest of the crowd visits and laughs from their positions within my yard.

"I'd say our first event was a big success," Jase says as he weaves his fingers between mine.

"I believe you would be correct, Mr. Bentley," I say as I lay back on his arm, snuggled in closely.

"I kinda like having kids running around the backyard," Jase says out of the blue.

"Me too," I reply, watching Brooklyn stand by Maddox and wave her sparkler.

"Maybe someday we'll add our own few to the mix," he whispers as he strokes my knuckles with his thumb on our linked hands.

"I think that sounds nice," I say, turning so my chin is nestled into his neck. Jase smells musky and hot with a little sweat mixed in. It's an aphrodisiac.

After about twenty minutes, it's finally dark enough for the first sets of fireworks to be shot off. The vibrant red, blue, green, silver, and gold are mesmerizing and breathtaking. Shot after shot after shot of glorious colors in all shapes and designs. I never appreciated fireworks until this year. Until I'm watching them from Jase's embrace.

Suddenly, he's rolling me over and scooting out from under me. He stands up so quickly that he almost loses his balance.

I sit up just as quickly, concerned that something is seriously wrong with him. He grabs my hands and pulls me up until I'm standing right in front of him.

"Jase, are you -" I start, but am cut off as Jase places his fingers on my lips, silencing me.

"Holly, I've had an amazing life and career. I've played stadiums and arenas that most artists dream about. I've been to countries that I never imagined I'd visit. I've done what I loved

190

since I was eighteen years old in front of crowds of twenty to thousands. Music was my first love, my only love, for so long. Until you walked into that room three months ago. From that exact moment, I knew you were different. I knew that music was no longer my first love."

Those green eyes pierce me through the darkness. "I fell in love with you the moment I laid eyes on you. You amaze me every day with your strength and your big heart. You are the most caring and nurturing person I know and that's evident every day in your work as a nurse and every time I watch you interact with Avery's kids. It sounds completely corny and a little cliché to say, but you complete me and make me whole. I am just a messed up, inadequate man without you.

"With that said, I'm still learning here. I know I'm going to make mistakes and I'm going to piss you off - maybe even daily. As long as you promise me that you won't give up on me, I promise you that I will continually strive to be worthy of your love. I will prove it to you every single day," Jase says, his voice cracking from the weight of his emotion.

I know Jase is standing before me because I feel his heat. I feel his eyes gazing so deep down inside me that he can see my entire soul. I feel the strength of his words. I feel it all even though I can't see him through my tears. I can't speak through the lump in my throat, but I know that my words aren't needed right now.

Jase reaches up and wipes my tears with the pads of his thumbs as the fireworks explode high in the clear night sky around us.

"I have something for you," he whispers as he reaches into the front pocket on his khaki shorts and pulls out a little black velvet bag.

"This actually belonged to my grandmother," he says as he drops the beautiful solitaire square diamond on a white gold band into his hand. It's the perfect size for me - not too big so that it wouldn't get in the way at work.

"I told you last month that I would be doing this one day. I just didn't tell you that it would be sooner rather than later," Jase says moments before he drops to one knee. My heart jumps in my throat and is beating at a rapid fire pace. I practically choke on the breath that gets caught in my throat as I watch him kneel before me, my shaking hand still firmly in one of his.

"Holly Jenkins, my life is only complete with you in it. I pledge everything I have and everything I am to you. You are my music, my hope. Will you marry me?"

I can't even speak. Shaking my head up and down seems like even the biggest of chores right now, but I want nothing more than to scream my answer from the mountain tops.

"Yes," I whisper moments before Jase jumps up and pulls me into his arms. Warmth wraps around me as his lips press firmly against mine. This is that moment that every little girl dreams about while they're growing up, but the best part is that this moment is real.

Jase is my prince.

And this moment was better than anything I could have ever imagined.

Fireworks continue to burst in the distance, and I'm vaguely aware of the murmurs of our family and friends around us. I don't want to break off the kiss, but eventually Jase pulls back - joy and excitement radiating from his devastatingly handsome face.

His hand has a slight tremor to it as he slides the ring onto my left ring finger.

"You are my everything, Holly. I love you more than I ever thought was possible," he whispers against the side of my face as he slowly turns us to watch the rest of the fireworks. The grand finale is breathtaking. Though, I'd have to say our grand finale was better.

I watch the bright colors explode brilliantly in the sky, my arms wrapped firmly around Jase's waist. He places a gentle kiss on the top of my head as the crowd around us cheers at the end of the show.

"Promise me something, Holly," Jase says.

"Anything."

"Promise me you'll let me win a fight every once in awhile," he says with the slightest hint of laughter in his voice.

"If it means we get to have makeup sex, you can pick a fight with me every day and I'll even let you win a few," I sass back. "Promise me something, Jase," I add after several moments of taking in the scene around us.

He doesn't even say anything, just turns me to face him. The look in his eyes confirms that he would do anything I asked of him right now - in a heartbeat.

"Promise me that you'll keep writing beautiful music," I tell him.

"Oh, that's a given. You and me? We'll be making music together for the rest of our lives. I guarantee it," he says with another kiss.

Who would have known I would walk into a Meet and Greet and meet my future husband? Who would have thought I'd be featured in newspapers and magazines from all over the country? Who would have guessed I would have everything I could have ever wanted in this exact moment? Not me.

But, that's the crazy thing about life. It never goes according to plan.

Life is like music. It has its highs and lows, its fast paces and slow melodies. And like music, life is dramatic, agonizingly beautiful, and yet so full of love. It's full of hope.

I don't know about you, but I'm going to spend the rest of my life making beautiful music.

That I promise.

~ *THE END* ~

Lacey Black

Acknowledgements

I'm going to attempt to make this one short and sweet, but I can already see that's probably not going to happen. THANK YOU to everyone who took the chance on this Indie, unheard of author, and purchased this book! This has been an amazing ride and I still love what I'm doing every day!! To my fan club/street team, Lacey's Ladies, I adore you all SO much…Thank you for the daily smiles and for keeping me stocked on Nick Bateman photos! My beta readers and friends, Amanda, Sandra, and Taryn, and my editor, Emily…Thank you doesn't seem like enough, but THANK YOU! Ginny for my amazing covers and Brenda for your talent at formatting my books, thank you! Kelley for your help with the Blitz and Two Book Pushers for your amazing teaser pics! My family and close friends who found out recently about my "other" life! Thank you for your support, excitement, and love! To the real-life Holly…Best. Friend. Enough said. And to my husband and our little ones, you are everything! I love you!

All my love,

Lacey

About the Author

Lacey Black is a Midwestern girl with a passion for reading, writing, and shopping. She carries her e-reader with her everywhere she goes so she never misses an opportunity to read a few pages. Always looking for a happily ever after, Lacey is passionate about contemporary romance novels and enjoys it further when you mix in a little suspense. She resides in a small town in Illinois with her husband, two children, and a chocolate lab. Lacey loves watching NASCAR races, shooting guns, and should only consume one mixed drink because she's a lightweight.

Lacey's debut novel, Trust Me, was released in August 2014. It sent six weeks in the top 100 in contemporary romance on Amazon's Top 100 Best Sellers for e-books. Fight Me, book 2 in the Rivers Edge series, released December 2014 and was another Amazon Best Seller in contemporary romance, as was Expect Me, book 3, which released in February 2015.

Email: laceyblackwrites@gmail.com
Facebook: https://www.facebook.com/authorlaceyblack
Twitter: https://twitter.com/AuthLaceyBlack
Pinterest: http://www.pinterest.com/laceyblackwrite/
Tsu: https://www.tsu.co/LaceyBlack

Blog: https://laceyblack.wordpress.com